"CALEB, WHAT ARE YOU STILL DOING HERE?" JOY ASKED, her voice surprisingly husky as she watched him eat from a carton of ice cream with

He glanced a [...] forgotten where he was [...] de the car, and I di[...] ice cream. Want som[...] he fudge swirl and offe[...]

She shook her head. "No, thank—"

He slipped the ice cream-laden fingers into her mouth. "See? It's good, isn't it?"

Sweet and cold, the ice cream melted in her mouth. But even after she swallowed, the taste that remained was of him. Heat spread throughout her body as she watched two fingers full of ice cream disappear again into his mouth. Then he licked his fingers clean, his gaze meeting hers with such intensity that she wondered if he'd made a connection with what he was tasting and her. . . .

WHAT ARE *LOVESWEPT* ROMANCES?

They are stories of true romance and touching emotion. We believe those two very important ingredients are constants in our highly sensual and very believable stories in the LOVESWEPT *line. Our goal is to give you, the reader, stories of consistently high quality that may sometimes make you laugh, sometimes make you cry, but are always fresh and creative and contain many delightful surprises within their pages.*

Most romance fans read an enormous number of books. Those they truly love, they keep. Others may be traded with friends and soon forgotten. We hope that each LOVESWEPT *romance will be a treasure—a "keeper." We will always try to publish*

LOVE STORIES YOU'LL NEVER FORGET
BY AUTHORS YOU'LL ALWAYS REMEMBER

The Editors

THE COLORS
OF JOY

FAYRENE
PRESTON

BANTAM BOOKS

NEW YORK · TORONTO · LONDON · SYDNEY · AUCKLAND

THE COLORS OF JOY
A Bantam Book / October 1993

*If you would be interested in receiving protective vinyl covers for your
Loveswept books, please write to this address for information:*

Loveswept
Bantam Books
P.O. Box 985
Hicksville, NY 11802

ISBN 0-553-44301-1

Published simultaneously in the United States and Canada

PRINTED IN THE UNITED STATES OF AMERICA

OPM   0 9 8 7 6 5 4 3 2 1

THE COLORS
OF JOY

ONE

"Watch out for goodness' sake!"

Caleb McClintock blinked and focused on the young woman beside him who had just grabbed his arm and jerked him back from the curb of the grocery store parking lot.

"In our previous life the wagon train ran over you," she said, her expression concerned and more than a little annoyed, "and I *swore* I wouldn't let it happen again."

If ever he'd seen a woman worth being yanked from his thoughts for, she was it. In a word she was gorgeous—with waist-length white-blond hair tied back with a long red ribbon and lovely luminous blue eyes. "The *whole* wagon train ran over me?"

Joy mentally skimmed through a series of mild curses. She wasn't quite sure why she had blurted out the first absurd thing that had come into her mind. She supposed she could attribute it to the fact that seeing him about to step into the path of an oncoming Buick had startled her out of her own preoccupied state.

In other circumstances she might have admonished him to be more careful and then gone on her way, but a couple of things kept her where she was. First, very few people would have picked up the bizarre threads of her statement as he had and continued on as if they were having a perfectly normal conversation. In fact the average stranger might consider she was having a day off from the funny farm and get away from her as fast as possible. She couldn't help but be slightly intrigued. "The wagon train was in a hurry. We were running from the Indians."

"No kidding."

"Yeah," she said, looking at him a little closer. Extraordinarily sharp, pale-blue eyes gazed back at her through the lenses of wire-rimmed glasses. Surely his eyes couldn't have been that sharply focused a minute ago, she thought, or he would have noticed the Buick. "I always thought we might have been too hasty in making the decision to run. I mean, for all we knew the Indians could have simply wanted to welcome us to the neighborhood, us being strangers and all. But our leaders didn't feel that was exactly the right moment to stop and find out."

"I can see their point. I'm sure I did back then too. By the way, did the wagon train make it?"

Her curiosity grew. He had a cerebral, intellectual look, as if he might be a college professor, yet he wore a pair of faded jeans and a Metallica T-shirt, as if he were a student. His brown hair was just past collar length, without any discernible style, and every so often its ends lifted in the breeze. Some women, she supposed, might be tempted to run their fingers through its thickness to see if they could coax it to order. Some women might . . .

His frame was tall and lean with the long, taut muscles of an athlete who was involved in a sport that not only required strength but endurance. Except she had an intuitive feeling he wasn't the type who would be involved with sports of any kind. All in all he was *nice*-looking, she decided, in an interesting, somewhat rumpled and sexy way.

And while she had been studying him, he had been returning the favor. In fact his eyes were fixed on her with such intensity, their pale-blue color was now almost silver. She was used to men looking at her, but not as he was. His expression was so intent, so engrossed, as if he were trying to take her apart molecule by molecule and figure her out. She couldn't help but wonder, Would he bother to put her back together again after he was done?

"Yeah," she said finally. "The wagon train made

it. Unfortunately, though, that didn't help you any."

He considered her remark. "I must have been pretty much of a mess."

She nodded solemnly. "*Flattened* is the word I would use. You might have had a chance if it had been just *one* wagon—we had a doctor traveling with us—but as I said, the entire wagon train used you for traction."

He had seen her before, Caleb realized. And not in another life. Except . . . it hadn't been *her* he had seen, but someone who looked almost exactly like her. "I understand. Besides, you were all in a hurry, and I suppose you didn't feel you could take the time just then to see if you could help me."

"That's very true."

"Where were we headed?"

She was perfectly capable of spinning out the yarn indefinitely, Joy thought, and it was sort of fun that he was following her lead so seriously. Any other time she would stay and chat, but at the moment she had other things on her mind. This was her first day of assuming Grace's identity, and it had been so long since they had switched, she was really having to concentrate. In addition there was the added problem of running Grace's antique shop when she knew very little about antiques. Her nerves, she admitted to herself, were stretched beyond the norm.

"Let's get back to *flattened*. You do realize, don't you, that if I hadn't grabbed you, you would now resemble a pancake, because you would have just been creamed by a late-model Buick."

He cast a completely disinterested glance around the Saturday-afternoon bustle of the parking lot. "A Buick?"

"You didn't realize you were about to step in front of a car?"

"I hadn't noticed."

"I suppose that's good," she said, her guarded tone revealing she wasn't entirely certain if it was or not. "At least it means you weren't about to fling yourself in front of the car on purpose."

"I would never do that. Life is too full of wonderful surprises."

His gaze and husky voice left her in no doubt that he was referring to her. He made her feel . . . sort of warm and, well, *funny* inside. She couldn't remember ever being unnerved by any man. *Not*, she reminded herself, that he was unnerving her. No, her philosophy of men had always been that they were like pretty shells you found on a beach. They were made to be admired for whatever period of time you chose and then discarded for another, without guilt or harm to anyone. Why settle for one when you could have variety? "Look, just do me a favor. From now on pay attention! Your mind was obviously a million miles away. You must have been thinking about something really important." Was it another woman, she wondered, then frowned at her thought. What did it matter?

"Not really."

She wasn't sure she believed him. He obviously had a powerful world going on inside his mind. She stopped herself before she went one mental step farther. She could absolutely *not* get interested in this man. What he needed was a keeper, and what she needed were groceries, and as far as she could see, their two needs were not at all compatible.

"Look, just try to remember what your mother told you when you were little, and you'll be all right. Glance left, then right, then left again before crossing a street. Okay?"

"I don't remember my mother ever telling me that."

His silver-blue gaze was almost like a force, and she had the strangest feeling he was trying to pull her into the world in his mind. "She probably did," she said, deliberately looking away. "You just didn't listen." Unable to help herself, she looked back at him, then blew out a long breath. Heavens, he was *definitely* interesting. "Well, take care."

"Wait."

She stopped mid-turn, causing her hair to slide like a curtain of silk across her back. "Yes?"

"You didn't tell me where we were going."

"We?"

"The wagon train."

"Oh. We were going to California. It was nice back then. You would have liked it. There were no cars and relatively few wagons to look out for." She smiled and lifted a hand. "'Bye."

He kept his gaze on her as she strode across the parking lot, her bright hair swinging, the ends of the red ribbon flying, her shapely hips swaying, her long legs flashing beneath a short, bright-red mini skirt. The day was overcast, he noted absently, but she, whoever she was, had been like a ray of sunshine.

Actually he had been mentally working through a problem on a new invention when she had pulled him back from the curb, but as he stared after her, he realized the problem was now of secondary importance. Even after she disappeared into the store and he could no longer see her, her image, along with her bizarre words, replayed in his mind. He remembered the genuine concern spiced with more than a hint of annoyance in her eyes. It was as if, like him, she hadn't wanted to pull her attention away from whatever she had been thinking about, but she had obviously believed he had been going to walk in front of a car. What she didn't know was, he might have been absorbed, but he had long ago developed a built-in radar where objects were concerned.

He was tired from jet lag, but he couldn't stop the smile that curved his lips as he stood there, recalling every detail about her. And it was several minutes before he remembered why he had come to the grocery store.

He had a housekeeper who kept his pantry and freezer well stocked, but occasionally he got a craving for the odd bag of chips or a carton of chocolate milk. Or as happened today when he'd been driving home from the airport, fudge-swirl ice cream.

The ice cream was still a good idea, he decided, heading for the electrical sliding doors. He wasn't used to pursuing a woman, no matter how gorgeous. However, he couldn't deny he had suddenly acquired an additional reason to go into the store.

The inside of a grocery store was a mystery to him and therefore something of a trial to negotiate. It wasn't that he couldn't eventually find what he wanted—he could. It was just that grocery stores in the overall scheme of things weren't important to him, and therefore he had never bothered familiarizing himself with the layout of any of them. There were too many other, far more interesting things for him to think about. But contrary to what his housekeeper and most of the people who knew him thought, he was perfectly capable of buying his own ice cream.

And today, quite unexpectedly, he had an extra excuse to be here. And if he didn't know her name, he soon would.

What only a handful of people knew about him was that he could concentrate on as few things as he wanted or as many.

With one right turn and two lefts he found her in produce, surrounded by men. Chuckling to himself, he calculated the odds of four reasonably attractive, apparently eligible men converging in the produce section at the same time, and came to the conclusion it could happen only when *she* was also present. She was a luminous being who attracted men like moths.

"Here," one of the men was saying as he elbowed away another. He wore a rugby shirt and shorts that left his tree-trunk thick thighs exposed. "Let me pick the best peaches for you. I have a knack for finding the juiciest and sweetest."

He probably hadn't even had a game today, Caleb thought disparagingly. More than likely he simply preferred the way he looked in the uniform.

The automatic smile she gave the rugby-attired man told Caleb she knew exactly what the guy's intentions were but that she was totally unaffected, which made sense to him. If ever a woman had to be used to men hitting on her, it was definitely her. Obviously men had been falling at her feet since she'd been in the cradle.

"I'm sure you're wonderful at it," she said, "but I can manage."

"I see you're buying ground meat," a Ralph Lauren type said, nodding to the cellophane-wrapped package in the bottom of her basket. To Caleb everything about the man looked *too* pressed, from his jeans to, no doubt, his mind. But she didn't seem to notice as she threw him an absent glance.

"I happen to know a great recipe for beef Stroganoff using ground meat," the man said, persisting. "If you're interested—"

"Thank you. That's very kind of you, but no." She wheeled her cart away from the frustrated admirers to a bin of tomatoes.

A dressed-for-success man in a three-piece business suit pushed his cart into hers and then immediately adopted an expression of repentance. "Oh, I'm sorry!"

"Don't worry about it," she told the suit politely.

"Let me make it up to you over dinner."

She shook her head. "Thank you, but no."

Caleb couldn't blame any of the men. Even an absent smile from her was enough to make a man's knees go weak. He knew, because he had been the recipient of one of those smiles. But none of these men were getting anywhere with her. The thought gave him immense satisfaction. Unfortunately that left the question of how *he* was going to get her attention. But in the end he didn't have to do a thing.

She looked over, saw him, and with a concerned frown she negotiated her basket through the crowd to him. "You look lost. Are you?"

The smile she gave him was all the more power-ful, he thought, because she was so completely un-aware of its effect on him and the other men watching her.

"You definitely look lost," she said decisively. "Either that or you have a perpetual preoccupied air about you. In fact, now that I think about it, you look out of place. Do you come to grocery stores very much?"

"Not much."

"How do you eat?" Even as she asked the ques-tion, she realized that her interest in this man was coming way too easily. It was almost as if he was emitting some sort of invisible beam that pulled her to him whether she wanted to go or not.

He shrugged. "Restaurants. Room service in hotels. Friends. Sometimes even my housekeeper cooks for me, but our schedules seldom connect."

She stared at him.

His smile was enigmatic. "I'm not really lost. In fact I'm in the general vicinity of what I want."

"And what's that?" Again she had to ask herself

what in the world she was doing. When and if she was in the mood to spend time with a man, she'd find one. But right now she most definitely wasn't in the mood. *Especially* a man who could draw her to him and make her want to take care of him, apparently without even trying.

"What do I want?" he repeated, giving himself time to form his answer. Not that he was tempted to state the obvious. She didn't need another line thrown at her today or any other day. Besides he had never used pat pickup lines. He had never had to. "I want fudge-swirl ice cream."

She shook her head with resigned amusement. "I *knew* it. You are lost. You're not anywhere *near* the ice cream. You need to go five aisles over to the freezer section."

"Hey, good-looking!"

Recognizing the voice, she turned and smiled at the sandy-haired man in jeans and a flannel shirt who was currently passing through produce at a dead run, tossing items into his basket as if he were an NBA star and the vegetables were basketballs.

"Joy? Grace?"

Her hesitation was brief. "Grace."

"Hey, Grace, how have you been?" He scored another basket with a rutabaga.

"Great, Ivan."

"I haven't seen Joy in a couple of days," he said,

reaching for a head of cabbage. "Is she out of town?"

"As a matter of fact she is."

"Then why don't you come over for dinner tonight, and if Joy gets back home in time, bring her too. I'm going to make vegetable soup. There'll be plenty for everyone."

"Okay," she said, and completely missed the crestfallen expression of the other men looking on. "I will if I can."

"Great. See ya."

"Your name isn't Grace," Caleb said, his voice pitched low and directly to her.

With a mixture of astonishment and horror, she swung her gaze back to him. "Yes, it is."

"No, it's not. Who are you?"

She grabbed his wrist and yanked him behind a towering display of pineapples. "What are you talking about?" she asked. "How do you know what my name is or isn't? We've never met before today."

"You're right. We haven't. But a year or so ago I bought a seventeenth-century English-carved oak-paneled coffer from someone who looks an awful lot like you. Her name was Grace . . . something. Grace . . . *Williams*, I think. She had an antique store."

"Right," she said as calmly as possible. "That's my shop. You must have made the purchase from me. My name is Grace."

"No," he said as if he hadn't heard her. "Grace must be your sister's name."

"Would you be *quiet!*" She threw a quick glance around her to make sure no one was near enough to overhear. "All right. I do have a sister, but her name is Joy. We're *identical* twins, so I can understand why you're confused. None of our friends, much less a stranger, can tell us apart. Our parents can barely manage it."

"Then they're not paying attention. The two of you are not identical."

Her eyes narrowed on him. Now that she thought about it, *he* looked vaguely familiar. In fact she was almost sure she had seen him somewhere before, she just wished she could remember where. "We're definitely identical, and we have medical records to prove it. Now it's my turn to ask a question. Who exactly are you?"

"My name is Caleb McClintock."

"Who do you work for?"

"Myself. Why?"

"I—Never mind. Why don't you think I'm Grace?"

When he was truly interested in something, he could be endlessly patient, and now his tone was the epitome of patience. "Because I didn't buy a seventeenth-century English-carved oak-paneled coffer from you. I bought it from someone else. When we first started talking outside, I thought you looked familiar. Then when I heard you say you were Grace, I remembered her. My cousin and I spent a couple of hours with her one afternoon about a year ago."

She gritted her teeth. "Then if it was only a couple of hours, and a year ago at that, *how* could you possibly be so sure that I'm not Grace?"

"Because you look different. You're more the color of sunshine on a summer's day. Grace had a slightly paler tint to her, like the sun at dawn. And then there are your eyes. Hers were lovely, but . . . quieter. Yours are more . . . luminous."

Her mouth fell open. Quickly she closed it with a snap of her teeth. "That's the most ridiculous thing I've ever heard. *Luminous?*"

"You don't look at yourself too often, do you?"

"Every morning when I get dressed."

His smile was gentle, his voice soft. "Then you should see yourself through my eyes."

It just might be the most extraordinary thing any man had ever said to her, she thought, stunned. And it affected her more than she wanted to admit.

Because he was taller than she, he could see over the pineapples. "The natives are getting restless. The Ralph Lauren man and the rugby player are over there by the carrots jockeying for the next at bat with you. I think the Ralph Lauren man is going to win, but then, I'm not surprised. I figured the rugby player was all show."

She made no attempt to try to decipher what he was saying. She was too busy grappling with several astonishing facts, not the least of which was that he had known she wasn't Grace. She and Grace had different personalities, but no one had ever said they *looked* different.

"I repeat, if you haven't been in the shop for a year, and then for only a couple of hours, how could you say those things? I mean, most people can't tell us apart if we're standing side by side. And you expect me to believe you *remembered*?"

"I have a great memory for detail, depending on my mood and what else there is to think about at the time." He shrugged. "I must have been interested in your sister's shop. Either that or there wasn't much else to think about that day."

The amazing thing was she completely believed his explanation. Totally baffled, she shook her head.

"Besides," he said, "you caught my attention."

There was something in his voice that sent a quiver down her spine. "Have we met before?"

"I'm Caleb. Caleb McClintock," he told her again, then reached for her hand as if he were going to shake it, but instead he simply held it.

She felt oddly comforted by the feel of her hand in his. And excited. How stupid of her, she thought.

The two emotions didn't go together at all. "Caleb," she repeated, smoothly drawing her hand from his. "And we haven't met before? You're sure?"

"Not in this lifetime."

Temporarily nonplussed, she let her gaze drop to her basket. Caleb was not only strange, he had the most disconcerting eyes she had ever seen. They were like silver laser beams of concentrated focus. She made a desultory inventory of the contents of her grocery basket. Ground meat and peaches. Great. She hadn't even managed to pick out any tomatoes. With a sigh, she turned back to him.

"Okay, Caleb McClintock. Assuming you're right that I'm not Grace—mind you, I'm *not* saying that you are right—what is it you want?"

"Want?"

"To keep quiet about this."

"You don't have to give me anything to keep quiet about the fact that you're not Grace. But I do want something. Have dinner with me. We can have fudge-swirl ice cream at my house."

She stared at him. "That's all you want?"

"No, but we can order in Chinese or whatever. Or if you prefer, we can go out."

"No, I mean is that all you want from me? Dinner?"

"It's a start."

"Start?" She felt stuck in a groove.

"So will you?"

"No." She'd been saying the same thing ever since she'd entered the grocery store. On Saturdays it was a notorious pickup place for singles, so she usually tried to come during the week. Not that any of it bothered her. Normally she would have laughed and flirted with the men, giving as good as she got. Except that today she had encountered Caleb first, and much as she hated to admit it, he had stayed with her when she had come into the grocery store.

"No," she repeated, mostly for her own sake. "Sorry, I can't." She paused, then felt compelled to add, "And if you don't go five aisles over to where the ice cream is, you won't be having ice cream for dinner either." For one absurd moment she wondered if she should draw him a map.

He smiled again. "Don't worry. I'll get it. Who's Ivan?"

"A neighbor of mine."

"Yours or Grace's?"

"Will you *stop* that!"

"It was a natural question."

"If you're not trying to blackmail me, then I've got to go—"

"And if I am?"

She became still. "Are you?"

"No. Are you sure you won't have dinner with

me? I can promise you you'll love the fudge-swirl ice cream. I'll even add nuts and whipped cream."

"I probably would," she said broodingly. "I've never met an ice cream I didn't like."

"Then it's settled."

"Nothing is settled. I'm *not* having dinner with you." Lord but he bothered her. He was like an itch she wanted to scratch, but she had the feeling that if she did, she wouldn't be able to stop scratching. *Jeez, Joy, you're losing it.* She started off, but then irrationally stopped. "Don't forget. Five aisles over." She pointed. "That way."

"I'll remember. But tell me something. Do you need help? I mean, do you have a problem? I'm pretty good with problems."

Her nerves jumped. Up to this point she had thought those penetrating eyes of his were only *trying* to see inside her. Had he succeeded? And if he had, what could he have possibly seen? "*Me?* Caleb, I'm not the one who's lost or who almost got creamed by a Buick. Plus, let's not forget I'm the one who made it to California."

"Right, in another life. But in this life, today, you do seem to be a little distracted."

Only by you, she wanted to say. "Caleb, you don't even know me. Besides, who wouldn't be distracted with a walking disaster like you on the loose?"

A small smile played around his lips as he watched her head back to the vegetables. Wasting no time, Mr. Three-Piece Suit and the rugby player converged on her.

Caleb turned his basket toward the ice cream. Five minutes later found him at the bank of pay phones in front of the store.

"McClintock's."

Caleb smiled as he heard Molly's gruff voice. She could have run a marine battalion with no problem, but luckily for him she had chosen to be his administrative assistant. "Hey, Molly."

"*Caleb!* Where in the world are you? I sent a car out to the airport to meet you."

"I parked my car at the airport when I flew out last week."

"I know you did, but you hardly ever remember where you left it."

"Well, I did this time."

"Okay, but I still sent a car for you. Didn't you see a man holding a card with your name on it at your gate?"

"Nope."

"I suppose it's a miracle you noticed that the plane had landed. Tell me the truth. The stewardess told you, right? I swear the next time you go anywhere, I'm going to pin a note on your shirt, like they do little kids."

"Now, quit grumbling, Molly. If you didn't have me, you'd have to get a pet, and you know how much you hate small animals and children. Besides, I couldn't find my ticket, so I chartered a plane."

"The man owns five cars because he forgets and leaves them all over town," she mumbled to herself, "but this time he remembers the car, but can't find the ticket I personally taped inside his garment bag in the most obvious, most prominent place I could find."

"Molly? Would you like to talk to me now?"

"I dunno."

He grinned. She was priceless. "Listen, I'm about ten minutes away from home, but I've encountered a couple of little problems."

"Okay, lay them on me." Her resigned tone revealed that she had heard variations on the same theme many times over the last ten years.

"I locked my keys in my car."

"What about the spare key in the magnetic box under your right fender?"

"Oh, right. I forgot about that key."

"You want to go look while I hold on?"

"No. I'm sure it's there."

"Okay, you said a couple. What's the other."

"Is Chuck there?"

"It's a Saturday," she said gruffly. "Why would he be here?"

"I might ask the same of you, but I won't. Is he?"

"Yes."

"Ask him to delve into the computers and look for a DMV listing for Joy Williams. I need her address."

"The Department of Motor Vehicles is closed today." There was an inflection in her voice that told him she knew DMV hours were only a technicality to him, but that morally she felt compelled to point it out to him.

"Yeah, I know. Oh, and while you're at it, have him check for a Grace Williams's address. I'll call back in about five minutes."

"Okay, but make sure you do. And *go home*. By the way, Daisy called. She's staying in Austin another night, but she said to tell you she'd call you later on this evening."

As Joy exited the grocery store, a carry-out clerk behind her with her sack of groceries, she saw Caleb. He was leaning back against a car, his jean-clad legs crossed at the ankles, nonchalantly eating from a carton of ice cream with two fingers.

Joy hesitated. The man simply didn't add up. He looked as innocent as a kitten, but she couldn't shake the feeling that he was really a tiger in disguise.

The most boggling thing to her was that he knew she wasn't Grace. He *knew*, when no one had *ever* been able to tell them apart.

He had probably intended to blackmail her all along and had simply wanted to wait until they were both out of the store.

And to make the astonishing more absurd, just looking at him made her want to go to him and see if he was all right.

She changed directions and reached him just as his fingers disappeared into his mouth. "Now what's wrong?" she asked, and was surprised by the husky sound of her own voice.

"Not a thing. Want some ice cream?"

"Why are you still here?" she asked, a bit bemused. "You're not lost again, are you?"

He laughed, a deep sound that caused warmth to tingle along her skin.

"That's the second time you've accused me of being lost. I'm not, I swear. This is my car."

"Then why are you still here? Is this going to be about blackmail after all?"

He eyed her consideringly. "Just out of curiosity, what are we talking about? Money? Sexual favors?"

She swallowed. "Caleb, when you blackmail someone, *you* set the terms, not the person you're blackmailing."

"I've never thought about it before, but now that I do, I guess that does make sense."

Unlike their conversations, she thought darkly. "So?" she prompted. "What do you want?"

"Joy, I already told you I wasn't going to black-mail you."

"Then what are you still doing here?"

He glanced around him as if he'd momentarily forgotten where he was. "Oh, right, I locked my keys inside the car, and I didn't feel like waiting to have the ice cream. Want some?" He dipped two fingers into the ice cream and offered it to her.

She shook her head. "No, thank—"

He slipped two ice cream-laden fingers into her mouth. "See? It's good, isn't it?"

Sweet and cold, the ice cream melted in her mouth. But even after she swallowed, the taste that remained was of him. Heat spread throughout her body. Determined to regain some of her former aplomb, she conjured up a dazzling smile for the young boy who had carried out her groceries, gave him a dollar, and took the bag from him. "Thanks. I'll take it from here."

The smile was almost the boy's undoing. Several shades of red later, he finally managed a "Thanks."

All business now, she turned her attention to the door of Caleb's car. "What are you going to do about your keys? Would a coat hanger help?"

"Don't worry about it. I can get in."

"I'm not worried, but what are you going to do? I mean, are you going to break the lock?"

"No,—"

She shook her head impatiently. "You don't want to break the lock. That's an expensive car, and it would cost a lot to repair it. Do you live far from here?"

"Just off Preston Hollow." Once again two fingers full of ice cream disappeared into his mouth.

Most of the men she had gone out with in her life had had nice mouths. But Caleb's mouth suddenly had carnal thoughts dancing in her head. It was beautifully shaped, firm, yet soft-looking, sensual even, and the bottom lip . . . Her head swam, momentarily disorienting her. "That's on my way. I'll run you home. You probably have an extra key there, don't you? If you don't, you can call a locksmith and get someone to bring you back. Do you have someone who can bring you back?"

She paused as she realized she had just offered him a ride home. She wasn't used to censoring her words or her thoughts, but in his case it would probably be wise of her to make an exception. It would also be wise to avoid eye contact with him. His expression was as guileless as a choirboy's, but he was gazing at her and licking the sticky, sweet residue of the ice cream from his fingers as if in his mind he had made a connection with what he was tasting and her.

"Are you the oldest sister in your family by any chance?" he asked.

"What?"

"You seem used to looking out for people."

"I'm only three and a half minutes older than Grace." And she was *not* used to looking out for people, well, not men, at any rate. In fact men usually fell over themselves to help her, not the other way around. But this man—She always seemed to be the one helping him. She shook her head as if to erase the unsettling thoughts that threatened to form. "Do you want a ride home or not?"

He straightened away from the car. "If you're offering a ride, I definitely want it."

Her skin warmed and her pulse accelerated as she mentally did an erotic translation of his words. But there was no way of knowing what sort of translation, if any, he had used. He was looking around, apparently for a place to throw the ice cream carton.

She was intrigued. She had never seen a man look or act less as if he was making a pass at her, but she was fast learning that he could operate on many levels.

Maybe it was his eyes, which could turn intensity on and off like tap water. . . . Or maybe it was his hair, which made her fingers tingle to comb through it. . . . Or maybe it was his body, which she was sure had never seen an exercise machine but she sensed possessed hidden strength. . . .

Whatever it was about him, she had come to the conclusion that there was more to this man than met the eye. It would be dangerous for a woman to even blink around him, because if she did, she would surely miss something, and it just might be important.

TWO

"There was another reason I was still in the grocery store parking lot when you came out," he said quietly, then drew in a deep, silent breath. From the moment he had climbed into her car, he had been inhaling her scent. The leather interior of her car had absorbed it, a feat he would like to accomplish himself. Hers was a lovely, impossibly sensual fragrance, as if, naked, she had bathed in a dew-covered field of white flowers on a summer night and the scent had never left her. The image tightened his stomach and heated his blood.

She seemed to think he needed to be taken care of. Since he was as confused about his feelings for her as apparently she was about him, he decided to let the matter ride, for now at any rate. "Turn right at the next light."

"Another reason besides the ice cream and your

locked-up keys?" She was trying very hard to concentrate on her driving, but she was finding it difficult. She had carried men as passengers many times before, and her car was certainly not small. But Caleb seemed to be taking up a great deal of room. There was an adequate amount of space between them—she had surreptitiously checked—but it still felt as if his body was touching hers. And everywhere she looked, she saw something of him, such as his blue eyes or his mouth. . . . She saw him even when he was staring straight ahead.

Unable to stop herself, she glanced over at his legs. The faded denim of his jeans stretched across his muscled thighs and outlined the bulge of his sex in a mind-boggling shrink-wrapped effect. Her hands tightened on the wheel. The car swerved, and she quickly straightened it. "Where did you say to turn?"

"At the next light. Right. It occurred to me that I hadn't thanked you."

She had completely lost the train of their conversation. "Excuse me?"

"I was waiting to thank you for saving my life." He offered the reason rather glibly, but he wasn't convinced it was the truth. He liked to think that he was a nice person, but the truth was he couldn't remember a time when he had gone out of his way to thank someone who was almost a total stranger to him—no matter what they had done for him.

"Oh. It was no big deal." She took the right onto a tree-lined street where big houses sat back from the road and were protected by high brick walls.

"You might not think so, but I consider my life a very big deal."

"That's not what I meant." She glanced at him and found herself gazing straight into his eyes. For the first time she saw a hint of humor hovering in their depths. In many ways the humor was more unsettling than the intensity. She adored men with a good sense of humor, but then, she reminded herself, whether or not he had a sense of humor didn't matter. She was about to drop him off at his house and drive away, and by the time she reached the corner, she would have forgotten him. *Like pretty shells on a beach*.

"Anyone would have done it," she said, her tone deliberately dismissive.

"Maybe, but anyone didn't. You did. And I wanted to thank you."

"Fine. Consider me thanked. Are we close to your house?"

"We're nearly there. Turn left at the next street, and then left into the first driveway you see."

She gave his directions far more concentration than they required, and a minute later she was driving past two big iron gates and pulling to a stop in front of a sprawling, stately, two-story brick house.

"You live here?" she asked, eyeing it curiously.

"Sure do."

"All alone?" She had wondered before whether he had been thinking about a woman. Now it occurred to her to wonder whether he *lived* with one.

"All alone," he said, not making a move to get out.

"You must like a lot of space." Or be planning to live with someone soon and start a huge family.

He regarded her thoughtfully. "Yes."

"I see." She didn't really, but once again she reminded herself that it didn't matter. She waited expectantly, but he didn't move. "Well, good-bye, Caleb."

"Would you like to come in?" The invitation surprised him even more than his original offer of dinner back at the store. The first offer could be excused as a spur-of-the-moment impulse, but he'd had time to consider since then, and there seemed to be no rational explanation for this particular invitation. He had a mountain of work to get through tonight, and he was sure that if he thought about it, he'd feel relief if she turned him down.

"No, thank you." Something worrisome nagged at the back of her mind, as if there was a problem she should be aware of.

"Are you sure? My dinner offer still holds. I know I ate the ice cream, but I'm sure we can find something in the freezer."

"Gee, that's an almost irresistible offer, Caleb, but I've got to go." The edge in her voice surprised her. She couldn't remember a time when a man had ever gotten to her to such an extent. But there was something about him. . . .

"Where?"

"To my sister's." She frowned at her quick, automatic answer. Apparently all he had to do was ask a question, and she would supply the answer. "What does it matter?"

He shrugged. Then he reached for her hand and held it between his. Staring down at their hands, he murmured, "I'm glad we've met."

Even if she'd been able to think of something to say, she wasn't sure she would have been able to. How could such a simple statement make her insides feel as if they were being rearranged? More than that, how could such an innocuous act as holding her hand have her suddenly wishing he would kiss her?

She pulled her hand from his. "Good-bye, Caleb."

With a smile he lifted his hand and lightly touched her cheek. "Good-bye, Joy."

Her heart slammed wildly into her chest as she watched him open the door and climb out of the car.

What in the world was going on with her? His fingers had barely grazed her, yet she could still feel the touch. And why did she continue to have the nagging feeling that there was a problem she knew about but hadn't yet identified?

She watched him stroll around the hood of her car and walk up to the front door. Then he sat down on the top step.

A light went off in her head. *Of course!* She slammed out of the car, her expression accusing. "You don't have a front-door key, do you?"

"Well, I have one, but—"

"But it's locked in your car with your car keys. Oh, this is great, just great."

With a chuckle he straightened his long legs out in front of him. "Look, this is not your problem. You said you need to go. Go."

"How can I leave you here sitting on your steps?"

"Easy. Just get back in your car and drive away. I'll be fine."

Part of her was fascinated by him, but another part was appalled. Men didn't usually try so hard to get rid of her. "You certainly don't let the little details of life get you down, do you?"

"I've never seen any point."

"The point in this case would be that you could

go inside where presumably you'd be more comfortable."

The day had darkened, and the wind had picked up. Her red ribbons were dancing around her head, and her blue eyes were definitely perturbed as she looked down at him. Even though he understood why she was so frustrated, he couldn't help but grin. "There's a bathroom window around at the side of the house that I always leave unlocked, just in case."

"Just in case?"

"In case I forget my keys." He surged to his feet and came toward her. "So you see, you can go to your sister's and not worry about me."

Right, she thought, searching for the relief she should be feeling and not finding it. Why, she asked herself, did she get so emotionally caught up in his problems? A brief thought flashed into her mind: Did she really think that if she viewed him as incompetent, she would forget how her body reacted to him?

"Okay, well, then good," she said forcefully. "I'm glad. You can climb in, and everything will be fine."

"It'll be fine," he said, agreeing, "But I can't actually climb in the window. It's too small."

"Too small?" She didn't even try to stifle the dismay in her voice. "Then you can't get in the house—"

He held up a hand. "Wait. There's a nine-year-old boy who lives next door. He can fit through the window. Actually, crawling through and letting me in is how he supplements his weekly allowance."

"Then you're set?" The question was asked tentatively.

"Yes." He sat back down.

Her annoyance had faded. Now there was only resignation as she gazed down at him. "What's the problem, Caleb?"

"No problem. It's just that it's Saturday afternoon, and he plays soccer every Saturday afternoon. I have to wait until he comes home."

Her gaze rolled skyward, seeking inspiration. She felt like a fish that was being slowly reeled in and she didn't know why. In this instance she was the one who was standing on the bank, trying to get Caleb out of the water, or at least to the safety of his house. "Could I fit in the window?"

"Probably, and I appreciate your offer, but you don't have to."

"Never mind. Just show me the window." She watched him rise to his feet once more, noted the way the denim material stretched and moved across the interesting landscape of his lower anatomy, caught the soft laughter that danced in his eyes. *"Wait just a minute."*

"What?"

"You live here? I mean, you"—she pointed to the center of his Metallica T-shirt where SEEK AND DESTROY was written—"*you* live here in this house?" She waved her hand toward the two-storied splendor behind them. "No." She shook her head, answering her own question. "No, the house and you don't match."

Grinning, he slipped his hands into the pockets of his jeans. "Sorry about that, but it's definitely my house."

"Look, I know houses like this one. I grew up in a house like it. My grandparents still live in it—"

"Really? Where?"

"Two streets over—" Dammit. More information given. "You're not breaking in, are you?"

He stepped closer to her, so close, she could feel the heat from his body.

"All right, Joy, if it'll make you happy, I'm breaking in, and I'm trying to get you to help me break in, which, by the way, you've already done to some extent, since you drove me here. I would say that was definitely aiding and abetting."

She stared at him for a long moment. "That doesn't make me happy, Caleb."

He burst out laughing. "Then tell me what will, and I'll do it."

She tried very hard not to let his laughter affect her. But its joyous, carefree sound played along her nerves in a way that made other, even more disturbing feelings inside her come to life. "Okay, then what I want is for you to tell me the truth. The *truth*, Caleb. Is this or isn't it your house?"

"It is."

She believed him, she realized. She'd believed him all along. "I know we've never met," she said slowly, "but you definitely look familiar. Could I have seen your picture somewhere?"

"You mean like on a WANTED poster?"

"Something like that."

"Let me put it this way: As far as I'm aware, my picture does not appear on any WANTED posters."

She shook her head in bemusement. "As far as you're aware? Caleb, in many ways, you are the most unaware person I've ever met." Yet he could make her aware as nothing or no one ever had, aware of the way the wind ruffled through his hair, or the way amusement lit his eyes with intriguing lights, or the way his jeans hugged his lower body.

His eyes glittered. "I'm always aware of what's most important, Joy."

Thunder sounded in the distance. It was going to rain soon, she thought vaguely, and Caleb probably wouldn't even notice that he was getting wet. "Where's the window?"

"I'll take you there, but I'm going to say this one more time: You *don't* have to do this."

"I know." She wasn't certain why he engendered this need in her to help him. She just knew she couldn't drive away and leave him to the mercy of the elements, even though it was spring and the rain wouldn't be that cold. She had to be crazy. "If I can get you inside, at least I'll know you'll be out of the rain." She cast him a suspicious glance. "At least I *think* I'll know it."

The smile he gave her held mystery, along with humor. He took her hand and led her around to the side near the back. "I'll have to lift you," he said, pointing upward, to a window about eight feet off the ground that was open an inch.

"Do you think you'll be able to?" Her tone was clearly dubious. "That's pretty high."

Laughter deepened the blue of his eyes. "I don't know. What do you weigh? A ton? Two?"

She gave a sound of exasperation. "If lifting me is going to be too much for you . . ."

"I'll be able to cope. Will you?"

Was that a challenge she heard in his voice? "I was a cheerleader in high school. I'm used to being lifted."

"Then let's do it." He moved to her and put his hands on her waist.

Capable hands. Strong hands. And she felt the heat of his touch immediately through the material of her skirt. But before she could be alarmed by the rising temperature inside her, he hoisted her upward with the easy strength she had suspected all along. She reached out and gripped the windowsill to steady herself, then pushed up the window.

He shifted one of his hands to her bottom, and the heat flowed downward into her lower body. It had to be her imagination, she told herself. It *had* to be. She'd never felt anything like that when any of her various cheerleading partners had lifted her in the same way. She waited for him to give her the final boost, and when he didn't, she looked down at him and saw a new expression in his eyes.

Predatory.

It was the first thought that came to her mind, but one that made no sense. Caleb was no danger. Was he? No. Heavens, he couldn't even keep track of his keys.

Oh, she didn't doubt he could have whatever woman he wanted in his life—in his own, offbeat, thoroughly sexy way he was very attractive—but he didn't seem to want *her*. Even though he had had plenty of opportunities, and in spite of the rather casual dinner invitations, he hadn't made what she would call a serious move on her. In fact, she decided, if she thought about it too long, she might be insulted. "What's the problem?"

"No problem," he said, moving his fingers almost absentmindedly against one rounded buttock. "Just catching my breath."

The heat grew and intensified until she felt in danger of melting all over him, like sugar icing on a hot day. Fortunately before that transpired, he gave her a final boost, and she was in the window.

Rather than try to support herself with her arms, sit on the sill, and swing her legs around and in, she chose haste over grace and slid headfirst onto a sea-green ceramic-tile floor. The cool feel of the tiles soothed her heated skin and quieted her nerves.

She pushed herself to her feet, stuck her head out the window, and looked down at him. He was gazing up at her with the same expression he had had before, that of a hunter who had sighted his prey and was just waiting for the right moment to spring the trap. Impossible. The image simply didn't mesh with his laid-back, careless manner. Her mind had to be playing tricks on her. "Caleb, are you sure there's no one here? I hear music. U2, as a matter of fact."

"I always leave the stereo on."

"Can't you remember to turn it off?"

"I could if I wanted to, but I don't like to come home to a quiet house. Besides, it keeps the plants entertained, plus anyone else who might break in."

Why had she asked? "I'll meet you at the front door."

"Wait a minute."

"What?"

"Because I leave the window up, the bathroom has a separate security system from the rest of the house. There's a mosaic panel to your right, and beneath it there's a pad of numbers. Open the panel and punch in seven, four, nine, four."

She understood security systems and the need for them. Without asking any questions, she did as he said, then headed in the general direction of the front of the house. But along the way she took a few deliberate detours, and what she saw amazed her. It looked as if someone had put real effort, imagination, and personality into the house. She supposed that she had thought anyone wearing a SEEK AND DESTROY T-shirt would have a house done in "grunge."

But Caleb's house was beautifully if eclectically furnished and decorated, with imaginative uses of color and form. A mother-of-pearl mermaid reclined on a Chinese wedding chest. A wide hall was lined with antique pinball machines. In a kitchen that appeared to have been recently renovated, antique wicker baskets hung from the ceiling, alongside the baskets that looked as if they had come from the local discount store.

In the living room two plush sofas and a love seat were grouped around the marble-and-mahogany fireplace. A conventional arrangement, she decided, until she noticed the ceiling, which was made up of panels of stained glass. At the end of the room there was a large brass-and-mahogany pool table, and in an alcove a heavy porcelain, claw-footed bathtub sat, filled with cue balls. Brightly colored fish glided in a long aquarium that took up almost one entire wall. A coral, Victorian-style bird cage hung in the corner of the entrance hall, a stuffed cow in it. And everywhere—on the floor, furniture, and shelves—there were haphazardly stacked books, as if they had been left in the exact spot where he'd finished reading them. Along with the books were scores of legal pads with pens clipped to them, some with writing, some blank.

She opened the front door to find Caleb waiting patiently, an arm propped against the doorjamb.

"Have trouble finding the front door?"

She blessed him with a sweetly sarcastic smile. "I took the scenic route."

Amused, he stepped inside and punched a series of numbers on another security pad. "Like what you saw?"

"It was all right." There was no use giving him too much.

"So do you finally believe this is my house?"

"I wouldn't have crawled through that window if

I hadn't. My benevolence toward the 'detail challenged' only goes so far."

One brow arched. "The detail challenged? I'm going to have to tell Molly that one. She'll love it."

"Molly?"

"My assistant."

"Her job must keep her very busy. By the way, wasn't it foolish to tell me one of your security codes?"

"The code can be easily changed." He hesitated, considering what he was about to say, but then said it anyway. "Stay for a while."

She shook her head. "I have groceries in the car."

"We can bring them in."

She barely heard his suggestion, she was staring so hard at him, mentally sorting through categories, trying to find a slot to put him in. She failed. "I know a lot of people in this area—like I said, I was raised around here. And of those I'm not personally acquainted with, I know quite a few by reputation. But I've never heard of you before today."

"That's not a problem, is it?" He took her arm and guided her into the living room. "I thought our past association was the only reference you'd need."

"Past association?"

"The wagon train—remember?"

"Oh, right. No, I just find it curious that I don't

know you or of you. But then I've been busy."
Thunder sounded again, only this time closer. Suddenly she found herself sitting on one of the sofas, and he was setting a match to an already laid fire. Then he was on the couch beside her, and in the background Bono of U2 was singing a romantic ballad. She must have blinked, she thought. How else could she explain it?

"I was raised in Michigan," he said as if she'd asked a specific question. "But when it came time for college, I migrated south. I liked the area and the climate. I also liked the fact that there was an airport here that could give me access to both coasts with relatively little trouble. I decided to stay. I've had the house for about five, maybe six years. I can't remember exactly."

More than ever he remained a puzzle, despite the fact that he had volunteered quite a bit about himself. Lord knew she had enough going on in her life at the moment, and there was no point in getting too involved with him, but . . . "What do you do?"

"I invent things."

"Invent? You mean things like those chop-and-dice kitchen doohickeys that are advertised late at night on television?"

He chuckled. "Yeah, something like that."

"There must be a lot of money in it for you to be able to afford this house."

"There's enough," he said mildly.

"I'm sorry," she said, immediately contrite. "That was extremely impolite of me." She had no explanation or excuse for her behavior.

"Don't worry about it. I wasn't offended."

"I guess it was just my way of trying to figure you out. You don't seem to fit—"

"Give me a chance."

His husky drawl brought color up beneath her skin. "That's not what I meant."

He eyed the pink tint with interest, then reached out and lightly brushed the tips of his fingers across her cheekbone. "A blush?" he asked softly. "Did you think I meant something improper?"

"You didn't?" She recognized a double entendre when she heard one. That's why she didn't understand her own confusion. In answer to her a smile spread slowly across his face.

"If you want," he drawled, "I can be very improper."

She just bet he could. "No. No, thank you," she said, then winced. She sounded as if she were turning down an offer to have tea.

He reached for a handful of her hair and let it sift through his fingers. The very casualness of his gesture revealed a wealth of control and experience, she realized. This man could find keys, women, a needle in the haystack, *anything* he wanted, *if* he wanted.

Oh, yes, there was *much* more than met the eye. "So tell me why you don't think I fit? By the way, I gather you're referring to my house."

"No, it's not the house. I like it very much. It's charming." And eccentric, exactly like him, she thought.

"Okay, if not my house, then what?"

She wasn't entirely sure herself. "I shouldn't have said anything. It's really none of my business."

He wound a strand of her hair around his finger. "I'm interested."

She shrugged. "I guess I meant I couldn't put you in a category."

"And are categories important to you?"

"They never have been before."

A slow grin spread across his face. "Maybe because before today you've always been able to categorize men, like the Ralph Lauren man today in the store or Mr. Three-Piece Suit."

She considered his remarks. "I have no idea what you're talking about."

"It's not always important that you follow along. There are other things just as important. For instance, what kind of music do you like?"

She had gotten entirely too comfortable, she realized. Here she was sitting on a couch with a man who wore a T-shirt that said SEARCH AND DESTROY, and she was strangely reluctant to leave him. Maybe without being aware of it she had entered a parallel universe. But where and when could it have happened? At the grocery store? In the parking lot?

She stood, and he immediately rose with her. "You're leaving?"

"Yes." She waited, expecting him to try to prolong their meeting, but he didn't. "It's been very . . . interesting meeting you, Caleb."

"I'll walk you out."

"No, that's okay. I found the front door once, I'll find it again."

"Joy?"

Already half out of the room, she paused and looked back at him. "Yes?"

"Thanks for the ride."

Lying in Grace's high, four-poster bed later that night, Joy was watching *Saturday Night Live* when the phone rang. "Hello?" she said, answering.

"Wow! I never expected to find you home on a Saturday night. I thought I'd get my answering machine."

Joy grinned at her sister's familiar voice. "Since I'm playing you for the week, I would have had to date one of your wannabe boyfriends, and I wasn't in the mood to be with any of them. Although Roger did want to take you to that new foreign film at the

Inwood you've been dying to see. Oh, and Jeremy wanted to take you to the Mansion for dinner. Both *veerrrry* tempting offers, I must say. But in the end I decided against either of them. I thanked both of them profusely, one at a time, of course, and told them you had a cold."

"And they believed you?"

"Sure. I was holding my nose when I was talking to them. They even sent me, or rather you, get-well bouquets. Very nice. Roger sent roses, and Jeremy a spring mix."

"I'll be sure to thank them when I get home," Grace said, her tone dry. "Anyway, so how did the first day go? Any problems?"

Joy's mind immediately went to Caleb. "Problems? No, but do you happen to remember a Caleb McClintock who was in your shop about a year ago?"

"No, at least I don't think so. Why?"

"I sort of, uh, struck up a conversation with him at the grocery store this afternoon." She omitted the part about the wagon train. "Ivan came whizzing through produce—by the way, he invited us over for vegetable soup, but I decided at the last minute to stay home. Anyway I told Ivan I was you, and Caleb, who was standing beside me, told me that I wasn't. Seems he made a purchase in your store about a year ago and can tell the difference between us."

"That's impossible," Grace said flatly. "No one can tell us apart."

"That's what I told him, but he says I'm like bright sunshine and you're like the sun at dawn."

"*What?*"

She bypassed the luminous-eyes bit. "Never mind. I don't think he's anything to worry about. At first I thought that Bertrand might be using him somehow against you. But then I got to know him, and now I would place a very large bet that *no one* uses this man without his permission."

"That's an interesting reaction for you to have and highly unusual. Ever since you saw the mayhem and carnage that followed after Mom left Dad all those years ago, you haven't let yourself get too interested in any man."

"You saw the mayhem and carnage, too, Grace."

"I saw it out of different eyes. No matter how much people think we're the same, we're not."

"Well, anyway, I'm sure I'll never see Caleb again. It was just one of those chance encounters."

"Maybe it's good that you won't be seeing him again. He sounds very weird, Joy."

She chuckled as she remembered. "Yeah, I guess he does." And sexy. And intriguing. "Oh, our grandparents called this morning. They're still having a great time in Monte Carlo."

"Did you tell them what we're up to?"

"Of course not. They would have felt compelled to lecture me, and with overseas phone rates what they are, I thought I'd spare them. Besides, I think we've already heard all their lectures on this subject."

"More than once," Grace said agreement. "All right, what about Bertrand? Did he make an appearance?"

"Briefly, but everything went okay. He stayed across the street in his own shop. We were actually both pretty busy."

"You didn't sell anything that wasn't already priced, did you?"

"No, I didn't, thank you very much. Oh, but I did let a customer talk me into selling her the George III mahogany cellaret for six hundred dollars."

"You did *what*? Joy, that was worth six *thousand* dollars."

"It was a *joke*, Grace. A *joke*. I may not know anything about antiques, but I do have some common sense. The cellaret is safe and sound with its price tag still in place." Joy grinned at the sigh of relief Grace gave. "So how are things going up there in upstate New York?"

"Fine. Better than I even expected. Getting the exclusive rights to sell the contents of this estate is going to be a godsend to my business, Joy, but I could never have kept it as quiet as I have without you. I can't thank you enough for doing this for me."

"Hey, forget it. What's a twin sister for, anyway? Besides, I can't wait to see the look on Bertrand's face when he finds out what you've done."

"Listen, are you all right? You sound . . . I don't know, funny."

"I'm fine," she said with what she hoped was conviction. In truth she understood Grace's concern. She *felt* funny, disturbed, unsettled. . . .

The Rolling Stones blared from Caleb's stereo in his upstairs workroom. He sat in front of the computer, staring at the numbers and letters on the screen, his concentration intense. When the phone rang, it took several minutes before the sound was able to fully break through his wall of concentration.

There were only two people who had his private number. One was Molly, and she never called after business hours unless it was critical; the other was his cousin, Daisy, the person to whom he was closest in the world. Still he answered begrudgingly. "Hello?"

"Miss me?" a lovely feminine voice asked.

Daisy. He frowned at the letters and numbers on the computer screen in front of him. "No."

The lovely voice broke into a laugh. "You're horrid, but I love you anyway."

"Ummm."

"Caleb, are you listening to me?"

"No." His fingers moved over the keyboard as he wrote another line.

"So you don't want to hear about what I did today?"

He leaned back in his chair, took off his glasses, and rubbed his eyes. "No, I already know what you did. You shopped, had lunch with friends, then later checked out the music scene on Sixth Street."

"Heard some great music. You should have been here."

"Next time." He paused to take a swig of bottled water. "So now I'll tell you what *I* did today."

"I already know. You flew back from Los Angeles and walked right past the man who was supposed to drive you home. I got an earful from Molly earlier today."

"Right. Except, that's not exactly the complete story. After I left the airport, I went to the grocery store and met a woman who saved me from stepping in front of a Buick."

"On your worst day you wouldn't step in front of a Buick or for that matter any other type of moving vehicle."

"The important thing is that she *thought* I might."

"Oh, I see," she said slowly. "So what happened then?"

"She drove me home, but she wouldn't stay for dinner."

"Well, how rude. And after you let her save your life like that too."

"I asked her more than once."

"Whoa! Are you feeling all right?"

Caleb smiled, remembering. "You want to hear something funny? She thought I needed taking care of."

"Doesn't she know you have a wall of people around you who do nothing *but* your bidding, which includes helping you deal with anything and anybody you don't want to deal with?"

"Nope. You want to know something else? She's really something."

She was silent for a long moment. "Do I hear a ripple?"

"A ripple?"

"Women usually come and go in your life, barely stirring your interest. It sounds as if this one's caused a ripple."

"Yeah. Maybe. To tell you the truth, I don't know. But I plan to work most of tonight and tomorrow. I want to have the details hammered out on the

new project in time for the meeting on Monday."
He paused. "I probably won't see her again."

"If she's that special, maybe you should. Listen,
I'll be home tomorrow afternoon, and—"

"Good. Stop by the store on your way in and
pick up some fudge-swirl ice cream. Two gallons."

"All right . . . Caleb? Do you ever wish we
could live like normal people? You know—fall in
love, maybe have kids, lots of them so that our two
families could have huge get-togethers? You know,
with kids and dogs playing on the lawn and me
taking home movies and you barbecuing something
wonderful for us all to eat."

He was silent for a long moment. When he at last
spoke, his voice was soft and filled with tenderness.
"It'll happen for you one day, Daisy. I know it will.
But I'll probably come alone to your get-together. I
lead a pretty selfish life, and I don't think there are
too many women who would put up with it."

"To lead a selfish life means you hurt people,
Caleb. You don't hurt anyone. You've just arranged
your life so that you can live it on your own terms,
and you're selling yourself short if you think there
aren't scores of women who would be glad to put up
with you."

He shook his head. "Even if this lady was the *one*,
she views me as an incompetent. In fact she called
me 'detail challenged.'" He smiled to himself, then

exhaled a long breath, deliberately dispelling the tension that had been building up inside him as they talked. "Even worse, I don't even know if she likes rock and roll."

"Good grief, sounds like a narrow escape to me."

He grinned as he heard the renewed humor in her voice. "Yeah, and besides that, I will never, *ever*, barbecue *anything*. Good night, baby."

"'Night, love."

THREE

Sunday dragged by for Joy, which was unusual for her. She was never at a loss for things to do and people to see, and she told herself the only reason she couldn't find anything interesting she wanted to do was because pretending to be Grace was hampering her.

Unfortunately she failed to make herself believe that particular white lie. There were too many precedents over the years where she had reveled in the game of fooling their friends. In fact she had previously made arrangements, as Grace, to meet some of their mutual friends down in the West End section of downtown Dallas for brunch. But at the last minute she called and used the made-up cold as an excuse, then spent the rest of the day brooding about Caleb.

Something about him made him hard to forget,

and she found the fact extremely disturbing. So she whiled away the hours going back over everything he had said and done, from the way he had smiled to the way he had touched her. And she ended up even more disturbed.

The problem was, as hard as she tried, she couldn't categorize him as just another pretty shell on a beach. No, he was too odd, too unique, too absolutely *maddening*.

In one way or another she had been joined with Grace since the womb. Growing up, she and Grace had been referred to as "the twins," when they were in fact two beings. As adults they had set out to create their own identities, with their own careers, homes, and in certain cases friends.

But Caleb *knew* who she really was. How? She felt consumed with curiosity.

What did he see in her that was special enough to make her stand out from her sister? Every time she looked at Grace, she saw her own mirror image. Yet, even though he had only met Grace once for a short time over a year ago, he had known she wasn't Grace.

There was something inherently powerful and fascinating about a man who seemed to know instinctively that she was Joy. Dammit.

Plus, every man she had ever been even mildly interested in had always asked for her phone number, but apparently the thought hadn't occurred to Caleb. Of if it had, he hadn't cared enough to follow through.

Of course she knew where *he* lived. More than once she even contemplated getting in Grace's car and driving over to his house, just to say hello and find out how he was doing. She told herself that doing so would be a strictly humanitarian act, considering that in the past, scores of people had died from eating food that had gone bad in the freezer. Hadn't they?

In the end, though, she convinced herself to stay home. Maybe she couldn't mentally toss him away as easily as she had all the others, but she would forget him. It was simply a matter of time. And after further reflection, she convinced herself that probably only one or two of the meals in his freezer carried some vile bacteria that would poison him. Chances were good he would choose one of the safe meals.

That evening, determined to put Caleb *and* his freezer out of her mind, she went over to Ivan's, who happened to be *her* neighbor, claimed she had a cold, just to keep in Grace's character, and scrounged a bowl of leftover vegetable soup.

Back at her sister's she took a pile of magazines to bed and read herself to sleep.

The next morning when the doorbell ran, Joy

was sitting at the kitchen table, her head buried in an article in one of those magazines. She was so engrossed in what she was reading that she carried the magazine with her, continuing to read as she padded barefoot to the front door.

Only as she opened the door did she tear her attention away from the article, and her eyes widened. "It's *you*!"

"I know," Caleb said simply, taking her in with a hungry, sweeping gaze. She had tied her long blond hair in a haphazard knot atop her head, and she was wearing an oversized Dallas Cowboys football jersey. The mid-thigh-length jersey showcased the lovely expanse of her legs right down to her toenails, which were painted a siren red. Normally he was able to shut out the world when he worked, but he hadn't been able to shut *her* out. The memory of her had played around the edges of his mind until it had been a wonder he had gotten any work done at all.

"No, I mean I know who you are."

Reluctantly he tore his gaze away from the contemplation of her toes. "You should. We introduced ourselves yesterday. May I come in?"

Almost without realizing what she was doing, she stepped aside, allowing him into the house. After pushing the door closed, she followed him. "I found *this*"—lifting the *Business Today* magazine she had carried with her to the door, she waved it in front of him—"on Grace's coffee table last night. I must have seen it somewhere before this morning. That's why I kept thinking I'd met you before."

He cast a disinterested eye at the artist's rendering of his likeness on the cover. "That's pretty bad. Maybe I should have let them photograph me after all."

Joy glanced at the drawing. "It's fine. In fact it looks enough like you to make me think that you looked familiar. It just never occurred to me that I might have seen you on the cover of a magazine."

His lips twisted wryly. "No," he agreed. "You thought you had seen my picture on a WANTED poster."

"You were the one who said that. And you also told me you were an inventor."

"What does the article say I am?"

"Don't you know?"

"I haven't read the article, and I don't intend to. I also didn't let them interview me."

"Why?"

"I have an aversion to having my bones picked."

"But they did the article anyway."

"Yeah, well, it's a free country. Is that coffee I smell?"

She wasn't sure. All she could smell was the clean, spicy scent of him. He was wearing a pair of black jeans and a hand-tailored black blazer, worn open over a black T-shirt that said GO SPEED RACER GO. The effect was wealthy, casual, and devastating. "Caleb, the article says you are an inventor."

"Right. That's what I told you. Did you forget? Coffee?"

She automatically shook her head, as if he'd offered her a cup. "But I thought you invented kitchen doodads. Remember? I asked you if you invented things like the slice-and-dice doohickeys you see on television."

Amusement glimmered in his eyes. "And what did I say?"

"You said, 'Something like that.'"

"Well, there you go, then. That's what I do."

Lightly, nonchalantly, he brushed his hand across her hair, but the gesture caused a quickening of heat in her veins.

"How did you get your hair in that knot?"

"I tied it, and no, Caleb, inventing kitchen doodads isn't what you do."

"No?" he asked as if he genuinely didn't know.

"No. This article says you're responsible for innovations in the fields of electronics, medicine, and telecommunications."

"Same thing, only the doodads and doohickeys are on a slightly different level. And since we're speaking of kitchens, is it this way?" He pointed toward a door and then sauntered off in the same direction.

She had no choice but to follow him. "*Slightly* different level? Caleb, if half of what this article says about you is true, then you're a genius."

"Really?" he asked, his tone inferring once again that he didn't know and didn't care. In the kitchen he asked, "Where does Grace keep her coffee cups?"

She pointed toward a cabinet. "It also says you're a true eccentric."

"The media loves labels, don't they? I personally hate them. That's one of the reasons why I didn't cooperate with the article and why I don't plan to read it." He poured himself a cup of coffee, walked over to the kitchen table and refilled hers, then pulled out a chair and made himself at home. "So tell me—and be totally honest—how do you feel about eccentric geniuses?"

His manner couldn't have been more relaxed, but she felt as if a tornado had swept through the house, upending everything, including her. She dropped down into a chair and gazed across the table at him. There was a smudge on the left lens of his glasses on the lower right-hand side. She wondered if he'd noticed. She also wondered if he knew how great he looked in black. GO SPEED RACER GO, indeed.

She understood so much more now. He was

obviously a man who could live life exactly as he wished. Therefore he chose not to deal with ordinary details so that he could concentrate on the extraordinary.

Suddenly her mind clicked back into gear. "What are you doing here, Caleb?"

"I came to see you. I thought I'd try to catch you before you went in to work. By the way, what do you do? I assume you'll be working at Grace's shop today, right? I mean it's only logical that if you're going to all the trouble to stay in her house and pretend to be her, you'd also have to take the charade one step farther and work at her shop."

She was so astounded by his unexpected appearance, so caught off guard by what she'd read in the magazine article, she wasn't sure what she wanted to ask first. To her further astonishment she heard herself asking a question that had very little relevance and betrayed much more than she cared to about herself. "If you knew where Grace lived, why didn't you come over yesterday?"

"I had a deadline on a project and had to work." He put his coffee cup down and stared down into the liquid. Then he looked back at her. "But staying away wasn't easy."

He had a way of stealing both her breath and any possible words with which she might answer him.

"What did you do yesterday?" he asked softly.

He sat very patiently, gazing at her with those remarkable blue eyes of his, waiting for her to say something, and she had to work hard to remember. "I stayed home most of the day," she said after a moment's thought. "Then I went to Ivan's."

"Ah, yes, the vegetable-soup guy. *Your* neighbor?"

She nodded absently. "Yeah, but I went as Grace."

"And he bought it?"

"Of course." Her brow knitted. "Did you have something from your freezer for dinner?"

"I don't remember."

Even if he did, at least he looked healthy, she reflected, irritated with herself for even wondering. He certainly didn't need her help or her care. "How did you know how to find Grace's house?"

"The same way I would know how to find your house. I had someone check the Department of Motor Vehicles."

"You—? Isn't that illegal?"

"They're basically open records." He shrugged. "Basically. They just have procedures they like people to follow. Unfortunately I don't follow procedures very well."

No, she thought, he wouldn't. A person who was capable of creating something that had never existed before wouldn't follow procedures or be able to stay within lines. But certain types of lines had always comforted her, lines such as boundaries, for instance. If everyone respected boundaries, peace in the world wouldn't be a problem. People would get along with one another, and no one would ever be hurt by another. Oh, yes, she *liked* lines. Caleb, on the other hand, probably didn't even realize there *were* lines.

He leaned back in his chair. "You know, even if I hadn't known that you don't really live here, I would have known."

"Excuse me?"

He waved a hand that indicated not only the kitchen but the living room they had just come through. "Dark polished woods, English chintz, and antique knickknacks—it's just not you. I see you living with lighter woods, absolutely no chintz, and keepsakes that are more whimsical than valuable." He paused, and his eyes narrowed in a contemplative fashion on her. "In fact I think the place where you live is yellow, red, and sky blue, if not in fact, then in spirit. You're primary colors, Joy." After a moment he added softly, as if to himself, "Joy is primary colors."

Emotion, breath, heat—*something*—was clogging her throat. Panic gripped her and held her mute. She had to wait for it to dissipate before she could speak. "How do you know that?"

"I have no idea. Am I right?"

"You're spooky, Caleb. *Real* spooky."

"Then I *am* right."

She cleared her throat. "You're not entirely wrong."

"The short red skirt you had on Saturday was yours instead of Grace's, right?"

"Yes." She had been so anxious about her first day at the antique store, she had inadvertently put on a skirt of her own instead of something of Grace's, as she should have.

"I bet Grace doesn't have one red skirt in her closet, does she?" The smile he gave her was sweet and completely irresistible. She reached for the coffee cup and drank almost half its contents before she remembered she took sugar in her coffee.

Caleb glanced at his watch, then slowly unfolded his length and rose to his feet. "I'm sorry, but I have to go. I was due at a meeting about an hour or so ago."

"You're over an hour late?"

"I'm not a great fan of meetings of any kind, except of course the meeting you and I had in the parking lot of the grocery store. Now, that was a meeting. . . ."

"But, Caleb, you shouldn't be late—"

He reached for her and pulled her to her feet. His warm breath fanned her face. "Let's make me a little later."

She'd received a lot of kisses in her life, but none of them came close to resembling this one. His mouth moved on hers in an unhurried, almost casual way, the pressure light, at times almost nonexistent. But somehow he still managed to find every nerve ending in her lips until the sensations spread and expanded, creating a heat that wound its way deep into her body.

He seemed to expend very little energy, but before she realized what she was doing, she stood on her tiptoes, wanting more. His fingers tightened around her arms, supporting her, drawing her closer to him, and for a brief, blissful moment he increased the pressure.

Then he ended the kiss, gently and so gradually, she wasn't aware of what was happening until it was over.

"Gotta go," he said calmly. "See you later." He paused by the kitchen door and sent her an easy smile. "By the way, you have very sexy toes."

Joy slumped backward and braced herself against the edge of the kitchen table. He hadn't even broken a sweat, yet he had created fires in her that she instinctively knew wouldn't quickly go out.

Toes? He thought she had sexy *toes*? As Joy went about opening Grace's antique shop, the remark replayed in her mind like a record that wouldn't cut off. Along with the kiss. Along with his eerie knowledge of her. . . .

She couldn't remember ever feeling so off balance. And for the first time since she had suggested to Grace that they switch places, she wished she hadn't. She longed for the familiar routine of her own shop, a funky boutique that she loved down in Deep Ellum, a colorful, high-spirited section of downtown Dallas.

Not that Grace's shop wasn't wonderful. Housed in a renovated building in a quaint, but definitely upscale area of North Dallas, it was congenial and gracious. In fact it was the exact opposite of her boutique. She smiled at the thought.

As she switched on the lights, scents of lemon oil, old leather, and potpourri wafted pleasantly in the air. With no thought to time period or value, antique chairs, sofas, and tables were placed in conversational groupings as if they were in a home rather than a shop. Fresh flower arrangements abounded along with dried arrangements and were placed among snuff boxes, candlesticks, and vases. Bureaus held silver mirrors and powder boxes. Joy smiled as she noticed a silver picture frame holding a picture of her great-grandmother. It was a sign of Grace's witty and expert touch.

Still, Joy yearned for the familiar jumble of colors and textures that made up her clothing shop, where colorful characters wandered in and out and rock music played rather than Mozart. She tried to settle her nerves by reminding herself that she couldn't have a better cause to switch identities with her sister. Unfortunately her attempt to reassure herself worked only marginally.

It was an hour later when she heard the bells on the front door tinkle as it opened and closed. Joy turned to see Bertrand Partington, the transplanted urbane Englishman who owned the antique shop across the street. Tall, silver-haired, elegantly gaunt, he was, as usual, impeccably dressed in one of his many suits from his beloved Saville Row. And he was the *sole* reason for her switching places with Grace.

She mentally came to attention and smoothed her hand down the skirt of the leaf-green linen suit she had pulled from Grace's closet and donned.

As he made his way across the store to the desk where she stood, Bertrand paused now and again to evaluate a piece of merchandise. "Good morning, my dear," he said as he drew closer to her.

"Good morning, Bertrand. Things slow over at your place?"

He smiled pleasantly while his eyes narrowed on the two ladies browsing in the far corner. "Just a temporary lull. I thought I'd use the opportunity to pop over and see how things were going here."

"That's very neighborly of you."

She had met him only once or twice before, since her shop was open the same hours as his and Grace's, but Grace had briefed her on his habit of dropping by to check out her merchandise and customers. She couldn't help but like him, and she knew Grace did too. Unfortunately he had a proprietary attitude toward the antiques business. He persistently maintained that Grace was simply not suited for the antiques business, and in sometimes amusing, sometimes annoying ways, he constantly tested her mettle. In short he was a charming scoundrel.

He gestured with his ebony cigarette holder, its cigarette unlit. He had given up smoking several years before, but he had never been able to actually give up cigarettes. "My dear, just because we're competitors doesn't mean we can't be civilized." His eyebrows arched. "And speaking of civilized behavior, I don't suppose you have a spot of tea brewed?"

She couldn't keep mischief from entering her smile. "No, sorry, but could I offer you a diet drink?"

His expression turned pained. "My dear, I worry for you. So many sodas are bound to be hazardous to your health." Without missing a beat he pointed with his cigarette holder toward a Federal satinwood sewing table. "And I don't know what you paid for this, but if you paid more than two hundred dollars, you got taken."

Her smile never slipped. "Really, Bertrand, you worry far too much about me. Most people would see it as jealousy."

"But then most people are bourgeois and know nothing about antiques."

"Snobbishness is a very unbecoming trait, Bertrand. I'd work on that if I were you."

He wandered over to the sewing table to eye the tag. "I see you had London's refinish this piece. How do you like their work? Any problems."

"No problems, Bertrand, but thank you for—"

The tinkling of the door bells cut off her words as a handsome man in a three-piece suit walked in the front door.

Joy gulped at the sight of one of Grace's suitors, then quickly yanked several tissues from a nearby box and held them to her nose. "Roger," she said, then feigned a sneeze. "What are you doing here? And with another bouquet of roses." Roses *again*. Grace really deserved someone with a better imagination.

With a warm smile he advanced toward her, holding out the bouquet of flowers. "I had a few minutes and just wanted to see how you were feeling. You sounded so miserable the other night when we talked, I was worried about you."

Bertrand's brow pleated as he turned an assessing look on her. "You didn't mention you weren't feeling well, my dear."

She accepted the bouquet with a small smile, but kept the wad of tissues at her nose. "It's just a cold, Bertrand."

"Nevertheless, you should think about closing up the shop and going home. One can't be too careful, you know."

"Just another example of you worrying too much about me, Bertrand. I'm perfectly capable of working."

Roger dropped a careful kiss on her cheek. "It doesn't look as if you feel any better. I'm sorry. I hope that these flowers will cheer you up."

"They're wonderful," she assured him, reflecting that as nice as he seemed, he wasn't for her sister. Grace needed more than careful kisses. She needed a man who could curl her toes, the way Caleb curled hers. "And it was very thoughtful of you, Roger, especially when I know how busy you are."

With a grimace Roger shot back his cuff and glanced at his watch. "Yes, I am, and I'd better get going." He gripped her arm bracingly. "Feel better, and I'll call you tonight."

"I'll look forward to it," she said, relieved that he

was leaving. Now all she had to do was get rid of Bertrand.

Roger walked out just as a stylishly dressed woman she didn't know entered. To her chagrin Bertrand beat her to the greeting.

"Mrs. Andrews," he exclaimed, every inch the charming Englishman as he walked to meet her. "How *nice* to see you again. And how very lovely you look this morning."

With a pleased smile the woman absently patted her back-combed and sprayed helmet of raven-colored hair. "Thank you, Bertrand. I didn't expect to see you here."

"Oh, Grace and I are great friends. I make it a point to check on her often in case she needs my advice on a matter that she doesn't know how to handle." He turned to Joy. "Isn't that right, my dear?"

With a clenched jaw she smiled. "Yes, and you're such an angel do it, because, as I've often told you, your efforts are so unnecessary. How can I help you this morning, Mrs. Andrews?"

"I'm looking for a gift for a close friend. I was thinking of something like a vase in the hundred, hundred-and-fifty-dollar price range."

She had made it a point to familiarize herself with Grace's inventory, but off the top of her head she couldn't recall one particular item that might fit the lady's requirements. "I'm sure we can find you just the right gift for your friend."

Bertrand laid a fatherly hand on Mrs. Andrews's arm. "On the off chance that you don't, stop across the street. I have an exquisite vase in amethyst glass that would be perfect."

"Really? Amethyst? Oh, I'd *love* to see it."

"Then come with me," he said, guiding her toward the front door. "I know Grace won't mind when it means you'll be getting exactly what you want."

Joy had to nearly bite her tongue off to keep from replying sharply. "By all means, Mrs. Andrews, go and look, but then come back. I wouldn't buy the first thing you see, not for something as special as your friend's gift. I'm positive we have something you'll like as well or even better."

"Damn," Joy said softly as Bertrand ushered Mrs. Andrews outside and across the street to his shop. She had let him win this round. She was going to have to do a whole lot better than that.

Leaning back in his big chair, with his feet propped on top of his desk, Caleb stared out the big window that showcased a spectacular vista that swept from downtown Dallas west toward Fort Worth. But he didn't see the view.

The people who had come and gone from his office during the morning had seemed to him as insubstantial and as inconsequential as wisps of smoke. He had looked right at them without actually seeing them. He had seen their mouths move as they talked to him, but he hadn't heard a word.

Every brain cell he possessed was totally focused on Joy.

There had always been women in his life—when he wanted and for the length of time that was convenient. Daisy had been right when she had said women had come and gone in his life without causing a ripple. Joy, however, had the potential to cause a tidal wave. If he allowed it.

No woman had ever disrupted his life or his work, but even though he was now smack in the middle of several projects that interested him immensely, he could think only about Joy.

She was an anomaly. Give him a problem and he could think his way through it. But when it came to Joy, cerebral activity held no enticement. He had kissed her, tasted her, and he found he wanted more, much more.

He had to make a decision about her. But then again, was there really a decision to make?

Joy smiled good-bye to a gentleman who moments before had cheerfully paid three hundred and fifty dollars for a silver Victorian biscuit box with a swan finial and four paw feet. Personally she wondered what the paw feet at the bottom of the biscuit box had to do with the swan on top of it. In her estimation the Victorians had been wild and crazy kids with very little taste.

A glance at her watch told her it was three hours until she could close. Since for the moment there weren't any customers, she decided to take a small break to catch her breath. And annoyingly, as had happened ever since she'd met Caleb, her thoughts returned to him.

She loved men; her life had been filled with first boys and then men. She'd always believed the more the merrier. That way everyone had fun and no one got hurt. When the man got serious, as happened more than she liked, she would simply have a very gentle talk with him and convince him that it would be best if they remained friends. With very few exceptions it always worked. She had a lot of men friends.

And none of them had ever rattled her . . . until now.

She was rattled, rattled badly.

She was in an ironic situation. Right from the beginning she had been intrigued because Caleb had known she wasn't Grace. But his knowledge meant that she couldn't have the comfort of hiding from him behind Grace's persona.

If *only* she could revert to being herself, but unfortunately her sister had the opposite view of men as she did. Grace was more cautious. That meant that while she was pretending to be Grace, she had to modify her behavior toward men accordingly. Joy gave a low groan.

She was off her stride, that was all. What she needed was a good bout of flirting to put her to rights. It would remind her that she could keep a man at arm's length while enjoying his company and emerge whole and happy without any harmful, hurtful results.

Several minutes later she had her opportunity when an attractive man in his early thirties walked in. After discreetly ascertaining that he didn't know Grace and had never been in the shop before, she proceeded to flirt outrageously with him. He tumbled, of course, and asked her out to dinner. She politely refused, but the small conquest made her feel slightly better.

Smiling up at him, her sweetness not feigned, she said, "Call me next week, Jack." Grace would be back by then, she reasoned, and Grace and the man just might hit it off.

As she was congratulating herself on her idea, she turned and started. Caleb was standing there.

"I didn't hear the bells."

"No?"

A predator who could sneak up on its prey without making a sound. Dangerous. Very dangerous.

"What are you doing here? Are you lost?"

"Is that the normal way you greet your sister's customers?"

His hair was mussed, and his glasses were still smudged, but he looked incredibly attractive. He had gotten under her skin as no man ever had before, she realized.

"Then you're here for antiques?"

"No, I'm here for you."

FOUR

Joy swallowed against a suddenly dry throat as she stared at Caleb. "What are you talking about?"

"You. Me. I've decided you're worth the disruption of my life."

"Disruption?"

"Of catastrophic proportions. I want you."

No subtlety, no finesse, just a bald statement that should have made her furious enough to throw something at him. Except he had said, "I want you," and ribbons of heat had tied up her insides, momentarily making it impossible for her to utter a word.

He smiled at her, a smile that showed understanding and an intentional sensuality. "Yeah," he said softly, "it's a surprise for me too."

"You . . ." She tried again. "You are absolutely the weirdest man I've ever met, Caleb."

"You think so?"

"How could I think anything else?" she asked, gathering steam. "You wear strange T-shirts. Your hair never looks combed. Your glasses are dirty. You get lost and forget your keys and—"

"And," he said, interrupting her in an even softer voice than he had used before, "you like the way I kiss you."

She was stunned into silence. With no discernible effort this man could confound and astound her. He moved, slowly circling her, as if, she thought nervously, he were trying to find her most vulnerable spot. Even more ominous, his eyes glinted a captivating silver.

"If you say you don't like the way I kiss you, I'll take it as a challenge. If you say you do, I'll take it as an invitation. Offhand I would say you're in something of a fix."

She turned so that even as he circled she stayed facing him, never once letting him get behind her. "And I would say you're dead wrong, because you forgot one other option."

"What's that?"

"That I don't have to say anything at all."

His smile grew wider and his eyes more silver. "I would take silence as an admission that I was right."

"If you did, you would be wrong, and not for the first time, I might add. Now, if you would like to purchase something, I would be happy to help you. Otherwise, please leave."

He reached for her, pulled her to him, and brought his mouth down on hers.

It was a Caleb kind of kiss, she thought vaguely. The kind of kiss that seemed like nothing at all, yet was probably at this instant peeling the polish off her toenails that he had professed to like so much. A Caleb kind of kiss was made up of different kinds of pressure, all of them subtle, all of them burning. It was also made up of brief, tantalizing forays of his tongue deep into her mouth, forays that made her gasp at the sheer eroticism. And most of all, it was made up of fire. Pure fire that seared and scorched until she wasn't sure there would be anything left of her when he was done. And ultimately a Caleb kind of kiss left her helpless and clinging until it was beyond her to draw away.

In the end she didn't have to. He did. And casually, devastatingly, he swept the pads of his fingers across her trembling bottom lip.

"I'll buy something now if you like," he said huskily. "You've seen my house. What would you suggest?"

Suggest? *Suggest?* Her mind reeled.

A vast night sky, glittering stars, a campfire, Caleb above her, hard and dangerous-looking . . .

She shook the strange images from her mind. Lord, what was happening to her?

The man was not only sometimes oblivious, detail challenged, and very weird, he was also exceedingly dangerous. Because she was just beginning to realize that he frightened her, something no man had ever done before.

She took several steps away from him and was thankful that he didn't follow. "You don't have to buy anything, Caleb. You can just leave."

"I could," he agreed, gazing with seeming interest at a pair of Regency ebonized-and-gilded armchairs. "But since I'm not going to leave, maybe I should buy something."

"I'm not going to sell you anything."

"Good," he murmured. "Then we'll have more time for kissing."

She didn't see him move, barely heard the words, and then his mouth was on hers again and she was drowning, drowning in sensation only this man seemed to be able to evoke. She forgot all about the fact that she was standing in the middle of her sister's antique store. She forgot that only moments before she had been trying her best to get rid of him. She forgot everything but the need building inside her that demanded she return his kiss with nothing less than a full-blown passion.

There was no thought in her head to stop the

kiss. No thought about the possibility of customers walking in on them. No thought about maintaining even a semblance of propriety.

There was only awareness of pulsing nerve endings and coiling heat. And most of all there was awareness of Caleb's hard body as it pressed against hers.

Her fingers threaded up through the thick, vital texture of his hair. He slipped his hand beneath her suit jacket to the silk camisole and then the skin of her midriff. His touch sent her senses rioting, and when she felt his thumb graze across the sensitive underside of one lace-covered breast, she almost came undone.

"Close the shop," Caleb muttered against her mouth, his breath hot and sweet, "and let's get out of here." His lips claimed hers once more in a brief, deep, urgently hot kiss before he gripped her arms and gently pushed away. "Joy? Will you?"

His pure-silver eyes glinted with a ferocity that sent her pulse pounding. She didn't doubt that she was seeing a predator, but there was something else too. His chest was rising and falling with a ragged rhythm, proof that he had been affected every bit as much as she had by the kiss.

"Will you?" he asked.

Her mind screamed no, but the words she spoke weren't in agreement. "All right."

As horror at what she'd said washed through her, she gasped. Almost simultaneously she heard the loud, throbbing bass of a country-western song coming from the back of the shop, followed by the chime of the door bells.

Hardly aware of what she was doing, she gestured vaguely. "The back door. I've got to get it."

He tightened his grasp on her arms as she started to move away. "Joy? Are you going to close the shop?"

Her brow creased as she grappled with the effort of trying to return to reality after the passionate, heated unreality of his kisses. "No, of course not. Even if I wanted to, I couldn't."

His hands held her arms fast. "And do you want to?"

The crease in her brow deepened as she thought about his question, but there was no doubt what her answer had to be. "No, I don't. Now, let me go."

"I'll let go of your arm," he drawled, and did so, "but I won't let go of you."

A river of heat chased a chill down her spine, and she hurried from the main part of the shop to the back section. At first glance Caleb had seemed so innocuous, but she had learned fast he was anything but.

"Hi, Waylon," she said, opening the door to a muscular, square-built young man in his early twenties who wore his dark brown hair clipped short on top and in front but long in back. He had received his name because his parents were longtime fans of the country-western singer Waylon Jennings. Joy knew this because Grace had told her when she had introduced him to her last week while she had been covertly trying to teach her everything she would need to know to run the shop. "What have you got for me today?" She glanced behind him and saw the monster-sized pickup truck behind him. "You're driving your own truck?" Last week he had been driving the company van.

"I told you I liked to whenever I can, remember?"

No, she didn't, which meant he must have told Grace. "Oh, right, I remember you saying that."

He sauntered back to the truck and lifted a quilt-wrapped object from the bed. Unwrapping the quilt, he revealed a small tea table. "None of Dad's delivery trucks have the stereo system mine does. Did you hear that baby?"

"I'm sure half the people on the street heard it. Garth Brooks, right?"

"Right." He gestured with the table. "All London's had ready for you today was the tea table. Where do you want it?"

With a wave of her hand she indicated the back room. "Just set it anywhere. I'll price it and get it out on the floor as soon as I have time." Which would be when Grace returned.

"Fine. Is there anything else you want moved while I'm here?"

Though technically Waylon worked for his father's delivery service, he also provided Grace's muscle, both in and out of the shop. "Not today, I don't think."

"Okay, then. Hey, tell that gorgeous sister of yours hello."

She chuckled. "Joy looks just like me, Waylon."

He grinned, his eyes twinkling outrageously. "Yeah, I know. So long." He swung up into the cab of his truck and drove away, taking his wail of country music with him.

She turned. Caleb was leaning against the jamb of the door that led back into the shop. "See?" she said, her tone defiant. "No one can tell Grace and me apart."

"I guess that's their problem. It's not, however, my problem."

She shut and locked the door and made her way back into the main part of the shop, taking care to give him a wide berth as she passed. She couldn't find a rationalization or a precedent for the situation she was in. Realistically there was no explaining what his kisses did to her. Realistically she also couldn't kid herself into thinking that the situation would simply go away.

And realistically realism was highly overrated, she reflected ruefully as she settled at Grace's desk and began sorting through the mail that had come earlier. She tossed the inevitable junk into the trash and set aside anything that looked important. And all the while she kept an eye on Caleb, who was wandering in what appeared to be an aimless pattern around the shop.

What was he thinking? she wondered. He looked a little lost, but she refused to let herself be concerned or fooled. Any man who could kiss like he did didn't need to be worried about.

She was the one who needed the care and concern. He had been more right than he knew, she reflected with disgust at herself. After only a few kisses she didn't simply *like* his kisses, she *loved* them. His kisses were a problem. *He* was a problem. And as far as she could see, there wasn't a solution in sight.

Out of the corner of her eyes she saw him stop at the Regency sideboard Grace had acquired within the last year. It was a beautiful and distinctive piece, a little over ten feet long with boxwood lines and rosewood banding. It was one of Grace's favorites, and she used it for the coffee and tea she kept prepared for her customers.

Following Grace's habit and despite what she had told Bertrand earlier, she had made the coffee and tea first thing. Now Joy watched as, after a long moment of contemplation, Caleb poured himself a cup of coffee. When he absently splashed the hot liquid over into the saucer, she had to resist the urge to rush over and blot it up for him. *Dammit, the man can take care of himself.* With a slight frown he then turned his attention to the silver sugar-cube container and reached for the silver tongs. But instead of helping himself to the sugar cubes, he regarded the tongs as if engraved upon them were the secrets of the universe.

Her nerves snapped. She bolted from her chair, hurried over to him, snatched the tongs from his hand, and, using them, grasped two sugar cubes and dropped them into his coffee. "There," she said. "Now you can drink your coffee."

He looked at her with the same complete and unnerving attention he had been directing toward the tongs. "But I don't take sugar in my coffee."

She jerked the coffee cup away from him, causing even more liquid to spill over into the saucer. "Fine, I'll drink it."

His eyebrows arched, but he made no comment on her agitated behavior. "Do you have sodas in the refrigerator?" he asked, pointing to the small refrigerator beside the table. At her nod he bent to retrieve one.

"Would you want to tell me why?" he asked when he straightened.

Had she blinked again and missed something? "Why *what*?"

"It's a question I have that I can't seem to get an answer to. Why is it that when we're kissing, it doesn't seem as if you want to stop? And why is it that when we're not kissing, you seem to take two steps backward for every step forward I take?"

No, she thought, she hadn't missed anything, and neither had he.

"If I knew, I'd tell you, Caleb. But I'm sorry, I don't."

He followed her when she took the coffee back to the desk and sat down. Perching on the corner of the desk, he angled his body so that he faced her. And he waited.

With a sigh she rubbed her forehead. She wanted to tell him to leave her alone. She wanted to tell him that if she knew the answer to his question, she wouldn't feel so mixed up inside. But his question wasn't out of line. His assessment of her reaction to him was dead on. And so he deserved that she at least make an effort to figure it out.

"In some indefinable way . . . as crazy as it sounds even to me . . . you frighten me."

Instead of being startled by her statement, he appeared thoughtful. "You're not talking about fearing physical harm from me, are you?" His sure tone indicated he already knew the answer.

She shook her head, took a sip of coffee, then set the cup down. "No, and that's about all I know on the subject. You're the last person in the world I should be afraid of. You may be able to create something out of nothing, but I'd be surprised if you knew how to tie your own shoes."

"I wear slip-ons."

She glanced up and saw amusement twinkling in his eyes. A reluctant smile tugged at her lips. "What's more, you can't even open your own soda." She leaned across the desk and popped the tab for him. "There."

"I would have opened it when I was ready to drink it, Joy."

Of course he would have. She looked away from him, trying to make sense out of her tangled emotions. Why should she be afraid of a man who engendered such a strong need in her to take care of him?

"Have you ever had a serious relationship with a man?" he asked.

She shook her head. "I've never been interested in having a serious relationship." A thought occurred to her. "Oh, heavens, Caleb, you're not getting serious about me, are you?"

He studied her horrified expression. "What would give you that idea?"

She subsided back in her chair. He was right. A few kisses did not a serious relationship make. She should know that. She should . . . except that his kisses were somehow different from the kisses other men had given her. She could handle those kisses, remain in control. But *his* kisses . . . "Nothing. I just wanted to make sure."

"You know what I think?" he asked quietly.

"No," she said dryly. "But after reading that article this morning, I'm sure there are people who would pay small fortunes to find out what you're thinking."

"Guess what? You don't have to pay a cent. I think we should simply spend all our time kissing. So far it's the thing we have the most success with, which, by the way, is great news. Based on that success, it's going to be absolutely spectacular when we make love."

"Forget it, Caleb. Lovemaking is serious, and I don't get *that* serious about any man."

"The first part of your statement is admirable, Joy. The second part is directed straight at me, and it's important you know that I have nothing to do with whatever has made you feel that way. It happened before me and has nothing to do with me."

She was expecting a lot of things he could have

said, but that wasn't one of them, and once again she was struck dumb. Fortunately at that moment the door bells tinkled as someone entered the store, and she was saved from having to respond.

But just as she was thanking her lucky stars for the newcomer, she looked across the store and saw who it was. Ben Myers, an up-and-coming attorney and a boyfriend. Instinctively she reached for the tissues. Then she remembered that Ben was *her* boyfriend, or at least he was one of the men with whom she had been going out lately. Her mind immediately went into overdrive, trying to remember if Ben had ever met Grace. By the time he crossed the store to her, she remembered that he had.

Aware that Caleb was watching with interest, she gathered her composure around her and rose. "Hello, Ben. What a surprise."

After a nod to Caleb, Ben smiled at her. "I've just been seeing a client in the area, and I took a chance on stopping by. I was hoping for a minute of your time. Are you busy?"

"Not at all. Are you interested in antiques?" With a look at Caleb, she picked up her cup and took a sip.

"No, I'm interested in Joy."

She almost spit the coffee back in the cup. "*Joy?*"

He nodded. "I need your advice."

She glanced at Caleb. The laughter she saw in the depths of his eyes made her voice sterner than she intended. "Could you give us some privacy, please, Caleb?"

"Are you sure?" he asked ingenuously. "I know Joy. Maybe I could help."

"That won't be necessary."

"Maybe he *could* help, Grace," Ben said. "He's a man and he'll know what I'm talking about."

Her teeth clenched. "Exactly what *are* you talking about?"

He spread his arms out. "I don't know what to do about Joy. I'm crazy about her, and there are times I think she's finally going to give me a chance with her, but . . . I don't know."

Obviously she hadn't been paying attention lately, Joy thought ruefully, because she had badly misjudged Ben's intentions. She should have given him her little talk *weeks* ago.

"I mean, we go out, we have a great time, she laughs, she flirts like mad, she seems interested, and then just when I think it's okay to try to get serious, she pushes me away, metaphorically speaking."

"I know just what you mean," Caleb said, his tone commiserating. "Metaphorically speaking."

Maybe she'd give up men altogether, she thought darkly, glancing from one man to the other.

Maybe when Grace got back she would look into a nunnery. . . .

"Look, Ben," she said. "I think the best thing to do would be just to back away and find yourself some other nice girl. I know that my sister really likes you as a friend, but the fact is, she just doesn't believe in getting too serious about any one person."

"But that's ridiculous. Look at how old she is. She should be ready to settle down by now."

"Marriage?" she asked, startled. "You're thinking of *marriage*?"

"Why not? She's gotten her education and has established her own business."

"Really?" Caleb asked. "I didn't know that."

Ben glanced at him. "Oh, yes. A shop down in Deep Ellum. You should go down there. She carries great, cutting-edge fashions."

"I'll do that."

"It doesn't matter how old Joy is, Ben," she forcefully interjected. "If she wants to live her life without getting too heavily involved with one person, then everyone should respect her decision. It's not a big deal. And Ben, believe me, you're going to find someone to love, someone who'll love you back. You're too nice not to. Unfortunately that someone isn't going to be Joy."

"Are you sure there's nothing I can do?"

"Positive." Damn. Usually she was more tactful. But pretending to be Grace while talking about herself with Caleb looking on with interest the whole time had been too much for her.

His expression downcast, he shrugged. "Well, thanks anyway."

"Ben, I'm sorry."

"That's okay. I wanted the truth, and you gave it to me." With a wave of his hand he left.

Blowing out a long, pent-up breath, Joy collapsed back in her chair. "Oh, Lord, I hate that."

"What?"

"When people get hurt." She rubbed her forehead. "Do you think I was too brutal?"

"I think you wouldn't know how to be brutal if you tried."

"He'll be all right," she said more to herself than to him. "I'll call a couple of friends and ask them to check on him. Now that I think about it, one of them, Sarah, would love to comfort him."

"Is that right? And who are you going to send to comfort me when the time comes?"

She brought her hand away from her face so that she could fully look at him. "*You?*" Funny, she thought, she couldn't think of a single friend of hers who would be right for him. "You won't need anyone to comfort you."

"I also won't need the speech since I've already heard it."

She frowned. "Why in the world are we talking about this, anyway? You already told me you're not serious about me."

"Did I?"

"Yes. Don't you remember?"

"It must have slipped my mind. All I can remember is that I was talking about making love to you. It's strange how that one thought seems to crowd everything else out."

A sensuous warmth curled in her stomach. She gazed at him, hoping that her expression didn't give away how easily he could disconcert her and make her imagine what it would be like to lie tangled up with him in bed, their bodies damp and straining together.

And in that moment she knew why he frightened her. He frightened her because *it would be so easy to fall in love with him*.

Her hand jerked, knocking over her nearly full coffee cup, sending the coffee everywhere. "Oh!"

"Did you get burned?" Caleb asked quickly.

"No, but . . ."

He strode over to the refreshment table and was back within seconds with a stack of linen napkins. He handed half to her. "You take that side of the desk, and I'll take this side." A short time later the desk was clean, with the exception of a few soggy papers and a stained calendar page that showed the current date.

Joy glanced at the page for the first time that day and gave a groan. "Oh, Lord, I forgot."

"Forgot what?"

"There's an auction tonight I need to make an appearance at."

"Why?"

"Because as auctions go, this one is going to be high-profile. It's a very posh affair at the Malcolm estate, and people in the antique business will think it's strange if Grace doesn't show up."

"Then we'll go."

"We—?" The tinkling of the door bells cut off her sentence. She turned to see a ravishing redhead with legs a mile long and eyes the color of sparkling emeralds. To her inexplicable annoyance, the vision of loveliness headed straight for Caleb.

"Hi, darlin'," the vision said cheerfully. "I thought I might find you here."

Joy's annoyance changed to something like dismay as she saw Caleb give the redhead a warm smile, wrap an arm around her slender waist, and draw her against his body. "Hi, sweetie. Having a good day?"

"So far it's not too bad," she told him, and kissed him on the cheek. Then, still held against Caleb's side, she turned her attention to Joy. "Hi, I'm Daisy."

"I'm Grace. May I help you?" Even to her ears her words sounded stilted, but for the life of her she didn't know what else to say. She was having to deal with a strangely hurtful sensation near her heart that had commenced the instant Caleb had pulled the gorgeous creature against him.

"Her name's not Grace," Caleb said to Daisy. "It's Joy."

Her eyes widened in shock. *"Caleb."*

"Joy, this is my cousin, Daisy."

"Your cousin? By blood?" Obvious doubt weighed heavily in her tone.

"More or less," Caleb said.

Daisy was a little more forthcoming. "We're not actually related by blood. My mother was once married to Caleb's uncle, Mike. It only lasted about a year. When my mother decided to get rid of Mike, Caleb and I decided to ignore the grown-ups and keep each other."

"How interesting," Joy said faintly, feeling not one bit better.

Daisy looked around her. "Your sister has a nice shop here. Caleb and I've been here before, and I've dropped in several times since then."

"How do you know it's my sister's?"

"Caleb told me." She slipped from beneath his arm and began to browse.

Feeling unaccountably betrayed, Joy gazed accusingly at Caleb.

"Don't worry," he said calmly. "She won't tell anyone."

"The point is, *no one* was supposed to know, and now two people do know, and I'm still not sure why or how it happened."

"And I'm still not sure why you're pretending to be your sister. Care to tell me?"

"No, I wouldn't. It's none of your business."

The door bells tinkled again, and this time an older woman walked in, an extremely *angry* older woman if her stormy expression was anything to go by. *What now?* Joy wondered wearily.

"I'm very disappointed in you, Miss Williams," the woman said, advancing on her. "I gave you my business in good faith, and then you turn around and sell me a fake Regency sofa table."

Joy started in surprise. "Excuse me?"

"You know exactly what I'm talking about. I paid a fortune for that table and was quite proud of it. Then this morning I had several of my friends over for coffee. My friend Margie, who is very knowledgeable about antiques, examined it closely and then in front of everyone proclaimed it a fake. I've never been so embarrassed in my entire life!"

Joy dealt with the public day in and day out in her own shop, and no matter how nice most of the people were, there was always someone who proved a problem. "Did you ever think that your friend could be wrong?" she asked politely.

"Margie is seldom wrong," the woman said with a huff. "There are times I wish she were, but she never is. She got down on her hands and knees and examined the underside of the table and found the faint trace of round saw marks. She said that's an indication of a machine-driven saw, which would date the table well *after* the Regency period."

There had to be some mistake, Joy thought, but for the present, the only thing she could do was to try to mollify the woman. Grace could deal with the matter when she came back next week.

She conjured up a smile that was both professional and reassuring. "I don't sell fakes, so this time I can say with complete confidence that your friend was wrong. However, since you are clearly unhappy with the table, I'll arrange to have it picked up and your money refunded immediately. I assume you have the sales receipt?"

In the face of Joy's confidence the woman began to look uncertain, but nevertheless she pulled the receipt from her purse and handed it to her.

Joy quickly glanced at the name. "Thank you,

Mrs. Emerson. Would first thing in the morning be all right for a pickup?"

"That would be fine. Look, Miss Williams, I'm sorry to make such a fuss, but—"

Joy held up her hand. "Please, don't think a thing about it. What matters is that you're happy. If you wouldn't mind, I'd like to call on you next week, but you'll definitely have your money before noon tomorrow." Grace had left some signed checks, so it would be a simple matter for her to make the refund.

"Very well, then."

"Good-bye."

When the woman left, Joy sank into the desk chair. She wished Grace was back and she felt very small for the wish.

She glanced around the shop for Caleb. He was with Daisy, their heads close together as they studied a silver tea set. Funny, she thought, but even though he and his cousin had discreetly withdrawn during the time she'd been speaking with Mrs. Emerson, she'd been aware that his attention was on her and her conversation.

She watched as Caleb chuckled over something Daisy said and casually draped his arm across her shoulder. There was no doubting that the two of them were unusually close. Their relationship was another fascinating facet of a man who, in her experience, defined the word *fascinating*.

Oh, yes. It would be a snap to fall in love with him, but she had no intention of doing so.

He strolled over to her, his gaze sharply penetrating. "Everything all right?"

She shrugged. "Fine. I think the lady should get a new friend. At any rate Grace will take care of it when she gets back."

"And when will that be?"

"A week at the most."

"And in the meantime you have to keep up the charade?"

"It's not a matter of 'have to.' It's a matter of '*want* to.'" She threw a worried glance at Daisy. "And please, Caleb, don't do anything to ruin the plan. This is something that's very important to Grace and therefore to me."

"I won't ruin your plan, and neither will Daisy, but I would like to know why you're doing it."

Her loyalty to her sister ran bone deep. The fact that Caleb had somehow figured out she wasn't Grace didn't change that. "Look, Caleb. What my sister and I are doing doesn't concern you."

"I don't agree with that. For better or worse, everything about you seems to concern me very much, but okay, I'll leave it for now. When should I pick you up?"

Her fingers itched to take his glasses and clean

the smudge away. Her lips tingled for the feel of his mouth against hers. "Pick me up?"

"For the auction."

She grimaced. "Oh, right. Look, I have to go, but that doesn't mean you have to—"

"You have to go where?" Daisy asked, sauntering over.

"To the Malcolm estate sale."

"Oh, I received an invitation to that."

"Really? I thought it was just for dealers or serious collectors."

Daisy shrugged. "A friend invited me. I haven't yet decided if I'm going."

"Joy's going. Let's all go." Before Joy could protest, he leaned down and pressed a kiss to her tingling lips. "I'll pick you up at seven-thirty."

FIVE

Caleb is late. Joy stared at herself in the mirror, frowning at her hair. The French twist didn't look too bad, she supposed. Grace would have viewed the style as businesslike and would definitely deem it appropriate for the evening.

Where is Caleb? Joy chewed on her bottom lip. She had dressed in a black evening suit of silk faille— Grace's of course. The small, multistone, bird-of-paradise brooch on the lapel was a sophisticated touch copied directly from her sister. Lord, but she wished Grace was here.

Could Caleb be lost? She frowned again at her hair. He had said he would pick her up at seven-thirty, yet here it was almost seven-thirty-five. Maybe she should have offered to pick *him* up.

Get a grip, Joy. She was overreacting in a big way, but she couldn't seem to help herself.

She snatched up a hand mirror and viewed the twist from the back. A French twist wasn't her normal style, and Caleb would know it. She didn't know how, but he would.

She tore the pins from her hair, brushed it until the blond length was gleaming, then contained the hair again, only this time with a black chiffon bow at her nape.

Feeling slightly more comfortable, she picked up her purse and walked into the living room just as the doorbell rang.

She rushed to the door and opened it. "Where have you been? Did something happen? Were you lost?" The words ceased as she took in his appearance.

Caleb was wearing a hand-tailored dark-blue, double-breasted suit paired with a plain white T-shirt. Given the function they were about to attend, his dress was slightly unconventional, but nevertheless surprisingly elegant and incredibly sexy. And when he smiled at her, her heart almost stopped.

"I'm sorry I'm late, but I couldn't find my keys, so I had to call for a car."

"A car?" She dragged her gaze from him to glance over his shoulder for Daisy. But instead of Daisy she saw a long black car with a uniformed driver standing beside it.

He strolled in. "I have the company's number programmed on my automatic dial. They're very good at coming on short notice."

She closed the door after him. "But if you can't find your keys, how are you going to get into the house tonight?"

"Daisy has several spare sets. She can get me in."

So he wouldn't need her this time, she thought, feeling stung somewhere deep inside her. Daisy would take care of him. "Where is she? I thought she was coming with us."

"Did you? You look extremely beautiful, by the way." He stroked his hand down the side of her neck while his gaze raked lower to the deep V of her neckline. "Do you have anything on underneath that jacket?"

Heat fluttered in the pit of her stomach. Living in her sister's house, wearing her clothes, working at her shop, Joy had felt the need for the familiarity of something of her own, in this case her short, red silk chemise. But it didn't show. "Caleb—"

"I hope not."

Beneath the silk of her suit and the chemise, her nipples tightened with involuntary anticipation. She had never considered herself a sensual person. In fact there were times in the past when she had been sure that when it came to matters of sex, she possessed a frigid temperament, not that the fact had ever bothered her much. But Caleb could arouse her with an alarming ease. It took only a few words or a smile on his part. Or a kiss . . .

As if he could see straight through the two layers of silk to her breasts and her now-aching nipples, his smile grew wider. And his words added fuel to the fire inside her that had begun to simmer.

"I like your hair," he murmured, "but I'll like it even more when it's completely unbound and trailing over me."

As if he had reached out to her, she swayed toward him. The image of his hard body and hers twined together almost undid her. She was twenty-seven years old and a virgin. Up to now she had been content and happy with her life, but lately, since she'd met Caleb, she'd had to accept that her body was growing restive.

Tingling nerves, heated sensations, and alien urges warred and grew inside her whenever she was with Caleb. And when she was alone, her body yearned unceasingly for him.

She cleared her throat. "I realize you don't bother yourself with a lot of life's little details, Caleb, but try to comprehend this one detail at least. You and I won't ever be in that position."

He gave a mock groan that held a large portion of both humor and indulgence, a combination that was hard for her to resist.

"Tell me you're not going to let your fear come between us."

"Fear?"

"You said you were frightened of me, right? I think it's because you're afraid that you're falling for me."

Bull's-eye. "That's ridiculous." She folded her arms beneath her breasts and gazed sternly at him. "It's obvious that you think entirely too much, Caleb."

"I'm not wrong, am I?"

His smile held a knowledge of her that made her feel transparent. She responded with sarcasm. "*You*? And that multimillion-dollar *brain* of yours? I'm sure think tanks all over America would fall apart if they thought for a minute that you could be wrong about anything."

He sighed. "Would you please forget that damned article?"

"Gladly. No problem." She hugged herself tighter. Forgetting the article would be a piece of cake. Forgetting the man, however, would be another matter entirely.

"Face it, Joy. For whatever reason, you're scared to death of a serious relationship."

"Most people with any sense are," she muttered. "And I can't believe anyone, much less you with your nonchalant lifestyle, would want one either."

"There are a lot of things I want, Joy," he said, his voice quiet and serious. "And everything I want is tied up with you."

"You're out of your mind." Her chest felt so constricted, she barely got the words out. "We've only known each other three days."

"In this life."

"Why do you say that?"

"You said it first. Remember? The wagon train."

"But I was only kidding."

"*I'm* not. There's no doubt about it, Joy. I'm out of my mind over you."

"Don't." She put her hands to her head. "I feel like I'm on *overload*, Caleb. You've got to stop talking like that. This is all just one of your eccentric quirks. It's got to be. You probably view me as some sort of . . . of new gadget to figure out."

His eyebrows shot up. "Gadget, Joy?"

She exhaled heavily. "Forget I said that. In fact let's forget everything both of us have just said."

"Sure," he said laconically. "I will if you will."

He had given in too easily, but she had heard the "catch." He would forget *if* she would. Right. Well, she would try, she reflected miserably, though she knew it would be a very tall order. She had recognized the danger and identified it, yet for whatever reason she still couldn't seem to tell him to leave and not come back.

She just couldn't. At least not right this minute. "We'd better go. I don't want to be late."

Relaxed and appearing very much in control, he slipped his hands into the pockets of his slacks. "It's all right. Daisy said the actual auction doesn't begin until nine."

Throughout her body, nerves splintered apart. "Well, isn't it wonderful how well informed Daisy is? I know my life is certainly better for it."

"Hey," he said softly, reaching out and lightly touching her cheek. "Daisy is no threat to you."

Shame came almost immediately. "I'm sorry. I really am. I shouldn't have said that."

"Don't apologize," he murmured, letting his fingers trail down the smooth column of her neck until his hand stilled with his palm curved around the side of her neck, his fingers resting just beneath the suit's collar. "It's nice to know you can be jealous."

She looked at him in surprised horror. "I've never been jealous before, but I guess that's just what I was being, wasn't I? How odd."

His lips twitched. "I don't find it so odd. I felt the same way when I saw you flirting with that guy in the shop today."

Her blood warmed, thickened, and slowed. She wondered if he could feel the increased warmth beneath his hand. "Did you?" she asked, her voice husky. He nodded. "He was just"—she shrugged—"nobody."

His blue eyes held heated silver glints. "I know."

She wasn't safe. She might not ever be safe again. She shook her head, trying to clear her mind of the disturbing thoughts.

"Listen, about tonight. Just remember, when we get to the Malcolm estate, call me Grace."

His thumb stroked up the side of her neck. "Sorry, but I can't do that. You're not Grace."

"Caleb," she said, gritting her teeth with the effort of fighting him on both a physical and a mental level. "Now is not the time to start being obstinate. Tonight is going to be tough enough for me. Most of Grace's colleagues will be there, and I know very few of them. I'm going to have to stay on my toes, so if you won't help me, at least promise me you won't hinder me."

"I won't hinder," he said, his thumb stroking back down her neck. "I promise. But I'd like a promise as well. I'd like to know why you're going to all this trouble. I'd like you to promise me you'll tell me why you're doing this."

"Does it really matter? I mean, when all is said and done, this is really Grace's show. Well . . . it *was* my idea, but it's for her business."

He dropped his hand from her neck, causing her skin to chill.

His eyes glittered strangely. "I remember you were afraid I'd blackmail you the day we met."

"Try not to blame me too much. I know in retrospect that it was probably a very strange thing for me to expect from you, but I guess it was just nerves about my first day at the shop."

"I'd never blame you for anything, Joy. Just as I hope you won't blame me if I decide to blackmail you after all."

Her eyes widened. "You *wouldn't*."

"Tell me, and I won't."

She didn't know how seriously to take him. Despite the short time she'd known him, despite the way his eyes were alight with humor, she had learned that he did pretty much as he wanted. And the next instant proved how right she was.

He lowered his head to hers and proceeded to give her one of his patented Caleb kisses that spread heat everywhere in her and left her dazed and clinging, a kiss so hot, it felt as if he had melted her down, then re-formed her into someone who wanted desperately to free her hair, tangle her naked limbs with his, and make love to him for a long, long time.

Worse, when he finally ended the kiss, the feeling stayed with her, refusing to go away. *She still wanted him.*

She spent the entire ride to the auction silently trying to put herself back together again in some form that she could recognize. She wanted to be herself again, the old Joy who took men and life lightly and who would never let a man get too close.

She still hadn't recovered when they arrived at the Malcolm estate. To her dismay the first person she saw was Bertrand, standing in the grand, marble-floored foyer, greeting people as if he were the host. Her personal life might be in turmoil, she told herself firmly, but she couldn't let Grace down. Hastily she fished the handkerchief from her purse and dabbed at her nose.

"My dear," Bertrand said, coming up to them, dramatically brandishing his ebony cigarette holder, "I didn't expect to see you here tonight. With that cold you really should have stayed at home."

"I'm sure you're right," she said, smiling sweetly and speaking in what she hoped were nasal tones, "but I didn't want to miss the sale. Besides, I'm almost positive I'm not contagious." Just to be contrary, she faked a loud sneeze.

He took a couple of steps away from her, his expression close to appalled. However, Bertrand was nothing if not quick. Recovering, he turned to Caleb with an outstretched hand. "How do you do. I'm Bertrand Partington. I own the antique shop across the street from Grace's. I've been there twenty-five years now."

With an easy smile Caleb shook the older man's hand. "Caleb McClintock."

Bertrand's cigarette holder stilled. "*Really?* I just read your article in *Business Today*."

Great. On the one night she really needed to keep a low profile, she was with someone everyone knew of.

"It wasn't *my* article," Caleb murmured.

Bertrand nodded sympathetically. "I understand you didn't cooperate. Still, it was a very flattering article. Your work sounds fascinating. You know, you really should pop in to see me sometime. I have some marvelous things."

Joy rolled her eyes at Bertrand's blatant attempt to steal yet another customer, or at least someone he regarded as a customer.

"I'm very satisfied with Grace's shop," Caleb said.

"I see." Bertrand took a drag on the cigarette holder, seeming not to realize the cigarette wasn't lit. "Well, Mr. McClintock, to what do we owe the honor of having you with us tonight?"

Caleb reached out for her and pulled her to his side, letting his actions speak instead of his words.

Bertrand studied her with new interest. "You must have your eye on some of the things here tonight, Grace, to come out in your condition. Perhaps something for Mr. McClintock?"

"Ummm," she said in a noncommittal tone she hoped would drive him crazy. "What about you?"

"There are a few things I thought I'd take a look at." He leafed through the catalog, stopped at a page, and held it up to show them a large four-poster, canopied and draped bed. "Did you see this piece?" he asked, a hint of disdain in his voice. "It's quite magnificent, but it's a one-of-a-kind piece that I'm not sure would pay out for a dealer. The opening price is prohibitive, plus it would take up far too much space in a shop, *any* shop."

Bertrand was going to bid on the bed, Joy thought with a flash of insight. And he was talking it down in case she was also interested. Although he didn't know it, he didn't have a thing to worry about. The bed was not one of the items Grace had asked her to bid on, but it wouldn't hurt Bertrand to worry for a little while.

"I think I'll go take a look at it," she said, and noted that his complexion paled a shade. She couldn't help but grin. "See you when the auction starts."

The organizers of the auction had set up rooms for viewing the items that were to be auctioned. In her purse Joy had the catalog clearly marked with the items Grace was interested in along with the ceiling price that should be bid.

But for appearances she made a show of studying several pieces. She stopped in front of a George II solid-walnut chest of drawers, crossbanded in padauk wood.

"How old is this piece?" Caleb asked, coming up behind her.

The length of her back perceptibly heated as it absorbed his body heat. Studiously she consulted the catalog. "It's dated 1725."

"It's interesting, isn't it? I mean, for all we know, that chest could have been in our home in another time."

Her head came up, and she glanced over her shoulder at him. "What are you talking about?"

He shrugged. "If we were together on a wagon train that was going west to California, and we're together now, it's conceivable we could have been together in yet another time."

He fingered her chiffon bow. Though he wasn't actually touching *her*, her pulses still quickened.

"What do you think?" he asked softly.

"I've said it before," she said as levelly as possible, "and I'll say it again. I was only kidding about the wagon train."

He looked back at the chest. "Maybe you're

right about us not owning this. I'm not really picking up any familiar vibes from it."

Shaking her head, she moved on through the viewing rooms, bestowing on everyone a neutral smile that she hoped said, *I know you, but I'm really too busy to chat*. She didn't stop again until she was standing before a display of chandeliers. One of them in particular interested her. A check with the catalog told her it was a Louis XV ormolu, cut-glass, and rock-crystal chandelier from the mid-eighteenth century.

"Do you like it?" Caleb asked, his voice pitched so that only she could hear him, one hand coming out to rest on her waist.

"What's not to like?" she asked in the same low tone, but then gave a light laugh. "It's valued at twenty-five thousand to thirty thousand dollars, and I can see why. It's fantastic."

He stared at it for a minute. "I think we danced beneath it."

"Caleb, don't be silly—"

His hand tightened a fraction on her waist. "Don't you feel it?" he asked, his breath stirring her hair. "It seems to me you were wearing an extravagant gown made of yards and yards of gold silk, layered with a delicate lace. It had a low neckline that heated my blood, and I held you as close as I dared as we danced to the music."

The image sprang full blown into her mind, the two of them gliding across a polished ballroom floor while the chandelier showered splinters of light down upon them.

His hand left her waistline, and as he had back at Grace's house, he slipped one hand around her neck and let his fingers dip intimately beneath the collar to her bare skin. Delicious sensations shivered through her, and she was barely able to stifle a moan.

He leaned his head close to hers and whispered in her ear. "And I think I couldn't take my eyes off of you. I was mesmerized by you, just as I am now."

It took her several long moments before she could even draw a breath. She badly needed to get away from the chandelier and look at something else, she realized, something else that wouldn't conjure up seductive images in her mind.

Ultimately it was Bertrand, moving across her line of vision who propelled her into action. She forced purpose into her voice. "I need to go upstairs and look at the bed." She was rewarded for her efforts by a frown from Bertrand.

But before she took a step, a man she had never seen before walked up to her, a smile on his face. *Grace knows this man*, she thought in panic. To her immense relief Caleb must have sensed her predicament, because he held out his hand and introduced himself. "Caleb McClintock."

"Robert London," the man replied congenially. "My company has recently started doing the refinishing work for Grace's shop, along with several of the other dealers here tonight."

Joy gave silent thanks to Caleb for the information. Robert London was a handsome man with intelligent brown eyes, and from the way he was looking at her, she guessed he was a little attracted to Grace. "And he and his employees are the best at what they do," she said to Caleb. Grace had told her that.

"How did you like what we did with your tea table?" he asked.

"It was perfect," she assured him, though she had hardly glanced at it when Waylon had delivered it. "Listen, Robert, I hate to run, but there's one more thing I want to see before the auction begins. Could you excuse us?"

"Of course. I need to have a word with Bertrand anyway, and he's right over there. See you later."

A young man, wearing a tag that identified him as an employee of the auction house greeted them at the foot of the stairway. "I'm sorry, but we're about to close off the upstairs area." He held one end of a velvet rope as evidence of his preparation.

Joy smiled sweetly at him. "Give us five minutes, okay?"

He blushed and nodded. "Five minutes will be fine."

"Are you really interested in the bed?" Caleb asked her, as they climbed the winding stairway to the second floor.

She cleared her throat in an attempt to relieve the dryness. Pretending to be Grace while at the same time having to deal with Caleb had become way too strenuous. "Not really."

"Then why did you say you were?"

"Just to annoy Bertrand. There's no point in making it too easy for him."

"I gather he's a competitor of Grace's?"

She gave a short laugh. "He must have invented the word *competitive*. Ever since Grace moved in across the street from him five years ago, he's watched her like a hawk. He's from the school of thought that antiques are for *gentlemen* and are no place for pretty young things, who should have nothing more on their minds than their husbands and homes."

"You're kidding, right?"

"Not too much. He's very possessive of what he views as his place in the antique world."

"Why?"

"I guess it's just his nature. His certainly wasn't the only antique shop in Dallas when Grace opened hers, but his was the most exclusive and well known, with an elite clientele. He pretty much had a monopoly, and he liked it that way. Then along came Grace, young, energetic, with ideas and ambition. Her first business was from loyal friends of my grandparents, who, by the way, happened to be former customers of his. But then word began to spread, Grace got more business, and pretty soon Bertrand found himself having to compete for customers who previously had only come to him."

"Has he ever done anything to hurt her business?" he asked as they reached the second floor.

"A few things," she murmured, glancing at the catalog, "but then she's pretty good at getting her own back." Like what they were doing to him now, she thought with satisfaction.

Caleb smiled to himself. He didn't yet have the whole story about why Joy was pretending to be her sister, but something told him he now had part of it.

Following Joy into a large corner room, he received his first look at the bed. "Wow, I can see why they left the bed up here. You wouldn't want to move it too often. It must weigh a ton."

The huge mahogany bed had four thick, carved posts that rose to the ceiling and supported a lush, pale-gold silk canopy. Matching draperies fell in graceful folds to the floor and were closed across the back and one side.

Joy couldn't tear her gaze from the bed. "It *is*

huge," she said softly, almost reverently. "Some long-ago English lord must have had it built to his specifications." She consulted the catalog. "It says here that many years ago the Malcolm family found it in England, bought it, and had it shipped back to Texas." She strolled around the bed and experimentally drew the draperies at the foot of the bed so that the bed was now enclosed on three sides. "It's really wonderful, isn't it?"

His gaze on her, he nodded.

She laughed. "Everything Bertrand said about it was right. It is too big, and it will cost a fortune, and finding just the right customer for it is going to be very difficult. But my bet is he's going to set it up in one of the display windows and use it to draw people in. It's certainly unique enough to cause a lot of conversation." With her hand wrapped around a post, she swung around and perched experimentally on the ivory-and-gold silk spread. "It's even comfortable."

He sat down beside her. "I wonder why the Malcolm family is selling all of this stuff, anyway."

"I guess the heirs to the estate didn't want any of it. Either that or they wanted money more."

"They're making a mistake letting this bed go." He lifted her hand from her lap and pressed his lips to her palm. "I have a very sure feeling that two people could make spectacular love on this bed."

Suddenly she realized they were totally alone. The bed was the only item on the second floor that was to be included in the auction, and the other people in attendance who wanted to must have already viewed it. "Don't start, Caleb."

"You don't feel it?"

"Feel what?" She knew it was a mistake to encourage him, yet she was helpless to stop the question.

It seemed to her that Caleb barely moved, but she felt his hands on her and then she was lying on top of the bed and he was beside her. He reached out and pulled the last section of drapery closed, and then they were enclosed together in a silken cocoon.

He smoothed his hand across her stomach. "I think I've done this to you before," he murmured, his eyes silvery in the diffused lighting of their cocoon. "I've felt your muscles contract under my hands"—he paused as he felt her stomach muscles tighten—"just like that, probably in this very bed."

She tried to laugh, as much to ward off the effect of his words as his touch. "No, I don't think so."

"This bed, you and I lying here—it doesn't seem familiar to you?"

How could she possibly know? With his hand on her, rubbing back and forth across her lower abdomen, her thought processes had clouded. She shook her head, still trying to make light of the whole thing. "Don't tell me, let me guess. You think I was wearing a gown made out of yards of gold silk."

"Actually," he said, his tone extremely serious, "I don't think you were wearing much at all." Lying on his side, propped up by an elbow, his glasses laid aside, he slowly slid his hand upward until he could undo the bottom two buttons of her jacket and let his fingers stroke upward to find the silk that covered her. "I was obsessed with you then, and I couldn't get enough of you. Just like now. . . ."

She could feel herself softening, heating, beginning to want, to crave. "Caleb, this is ridiculous. . . ."

He unbuttoned the remaining buttons on her jacket and parted it, revealing the red silk chemise beneath it and her flesh to his hungry gaze. She shivered as the heated air touched the skin above her breasts and her shoulders, bare except for the delicate straps that crossed them. The air was heated by his breath and by the heat that was steadily growing inside her.

"We've been here before, Joy. Things were different then, time, circumstances, maybe even the colors, but you and I were the same, always. You were flushed with passion, and when I did this"—he skimmed his hand up her midriff and closed his hand around one breast—"you moaned with pleasure."

Unable to help herself, she closed her eyes and

softly moaned as her breast swelled to fill his hand. "Yes," he whispered, his head lowering to within inches of her skin. "Like that."

She desperately reached for her rapidly shredding sanity. "Caleb, the auction—"

His mouth closed over her nipple and suckled her through the silk, wetting the material, making her nipple tight and almost painfully sensitive. He pulled hard on the nipple, and she felt contractions deep in her womb.

"The auction," he said, his voice a harsh rasp of need, "can damn well go on without us."

He replaced his mouth with his hand, then moved to the other nipple, giving it the exact same treatment, until in frustration he thrust the silk down, breaking the fragile strap. But at that point she was too far gone even to protest. His mouth was on her, pulling at the tightly beaded peak with an intensity that bespoke a desperate, unending need. She threaded her fingers up through his hair and cupped his head, increasing the pressure of his mouth against her.

Her skirt had worked itself up her legs; her hips were moving in a rhythm she had no control over.

"Caleb." To her dismay his name was little more than a movement of the air.

Still suckling her, he slid his fingers over the portion of sensitive skin left bare on her upper thigh by the space between the lace-edged bottom of her panties and the elasticized top of her black stocking. The strokes of his hand were very sure, the pull of his lips impossibly erotic. She had never felt more vulnerable in her life, or more needy. There was a pressure building inside her that cried out to be released. From some distant place she heard voices. From some distant place she heard herself softly moan. She clutched at his shoulders, silently begging, but for what she didn't know.

He pressed the heel of his hand at the juncture of her thighs, and a shock of pleasure jolted through her, pleasure unbelievable, pleasure almost unbearable.

He caught his breath. He hadn't intended to go this far, but she was a combination of sugar and fire, and it was a combination he couldn't withstand. He had to get them out of there. But . . . with another muttered imprecation he settled on top of her. For one sweet, exquisite minute he needed to feel her beneath him, needed to press into her.

He rocked against her, pressing the hard ridge of his sex against her softness, gritting his teeth against the surge of intense need that rocketed through him. Then she began to move with him, threatening his resolve, his lucidity, his entire being.

Lord in heaven, if it was this good with their clothes on, what would it be like when they were naked?

"Caleb?"

Joy heard the voice, as she had the others, from a long way away. But it seemed familiar.

"It's Daisy," Caleb growled against Joy's ear. Desire for her had almost entirely taken him over. He hurt like hell, and her satin-skinned body promised him an ecstasy of release. They had to leave, but his need was almost stronger than his will. He rocked against her once more, pushing himself hard up against the place where her soft folds were hidden. He heard her draw in a ragged breath and knew she was close to climax. Calling himself every name in the book for getting them into this damnable predicament, he rolled off her.

She was a throbbing mass of want from head to toe. Her body screamed for satisfaction, but she could only lie there as pain pulsed through her. In the silence the sound of her uneven breathing mixed with his.

She didn't dare look at him. As much as she wanted him, she was afraid that one look from those silver-blue eyes of his and she would be begging him to take her. "What does Daisy want?"

His chuckle was low, harsh, painful. "Probably just to remind me where I am."

"She must have to do it often," she said dully.

He sat up and turned to her, his expression

almost fierce. "She's never had to do it before. *Never*. Okay?"

"Okay." She was grappling, trying to recover her dignity, along with her common sense.

He slipped his glasses on, then quickly buttoned her jacket and pulled her upright beside him. Bracketing her face with his hands, he looked deep into her eyes. "Are you all right?"

She tried to swallow, but couldn't. Despite everything, she still wanted him. "No," she said quietly. "I don't think so."

"Will you come home with me?"

She felt his tension as he waited for her answer. Strangely, after all the years of saying no, the yes came incredibly easy. "Yes."

With a gentle hand that trembled slightly, he smoothed back her pale hair. "I was right."

She had blinked again, only this time she didn't care. "About what?"

"We've been together in this bed before." He flung back one length of the draperies and pulled her to her feet with him.

Thankfully Daisy wasn't in the bedroom, nor was anyone else for that matter. The way they had been carrying on, she thought shakily, she wouldn't have been surprised to see the auctioneers selling tickets.

She arranged her clothes, pushing her skirt back

down her legs and straightening her jacket. Then she quickly retied the chiffon bow that not so amazingly had come undone. When she was finished, she glanced over at him and found him looking at her with a naked expression of desire so powerful, she began trembling.

Without a word he reached for her hand and led her out of the room.

Daisy sat on the stairs, her lithe body wrapped with a short, stunning white spandex dress, her elbows resting on the step above her, and her long legs angled downward over the next several steps below.

The velvet rope had been stretched across the bottom of the stairway. The young man had obviously taken for granted that they had come back down. *One more thing to be grateful for*, Joy thought.

Daisy smiled up at them. "Hi. Ready for the auction?"

If she'd had the strength, Joy would have hugged her for acting as if nothing had happened.

"Do you have my house key with you?" Caleb asked tersely.

"Sure do."

"Give it to me. Joy, do you have a list of the things Grace wants tonight?"

"Uh . . . yes, in my purse." Unthinkingly she opened her purse and fumbled for the catalog Grace had marked.

He took it from her and exchanged the catalog
for the key with Daisy. "Bid for those, will you, and
don't forget the things I've already decided on?"

Daisy stood and eyed them speculatively. "Sure.
I gather you two aren't going to stay?"

"You gather right." He dropped a kiss on
Daisy's cheek, then, still holding Joy's hand, drew
her down the stairs and out into the night.

SIX

Though with some part of her mind Joy knew she and Caleb had gone from the Malcolm estate to the car and then to his home, she was barely aware of any sensation of movement. It was as if movement had ceased not only around her but also in her. She felt frozen, not in temperature but in essence and in substance.

Maybe she was in shock, she thought, and if she was, deservedly so.

What had happened back at the auction wasn't like her at all. She *never* allowed things to get hot and heavy between her and a man.

Sure, she knew that a man could have sex without being emotionally involved, but she was positive she would not be capable of the same dissociation, though she had never tried out her theory. Consequently it had been a simple matter for her to avoid anything remotely passionate with a man.

True there were the odd moments when she would find herself wondering about that curious phenomenon that everyone called love. She would wonder what it would be like to love another person so deeply and so completely that you wanted to share the rest of your life with that person. And she wondered how it would be to always have someone to turn to in dark times and in light. But then she would remember that as a child she had seen firsthand what love could do to two people when it had destroyed her parents, and so the moments would quickly pass.

But the question remained. What had happened to her back at the Malcolm estate?

Okay, so she was playing the part of Grace. But practically making love to a man with a good half of her colleagues a stone's throw away wasn't like Grace either. So if what had happened wasn't like her *or* like Grace, who was it like?

And what part was she playing now? The question frightened her because she had no answer.

She glanced down and saw her fingers wrapped tightly around a cue ball, and for the first time she became aware that she was standing by the pool table in Caleb's living room. Glancing around, she saw Caleb, leaning against a near wall, watching her. He appeared relaxed, patient, and very much in control.

Damn him and his control, she thought, and in the next moment corrected herself. She should be grateful for his control. *She* was the one who had lost control.

"I'm sorry, Caleb."

He shook his head. "I don't think I want to hear this."

She made a vague gesture with the cue ball. "I shouldn't have let it happen."

"Do you really think you could have stopped it? Or should I say, stopped *us*?"

"Yes, yes, I do. I should have—"

"What?" he asked, coming away from the wall and advancing toward her, his eyes glittering enigmatically. "You should have told me no? Why, Joy, when you wanted it every bit as much as I did?"

"That's probably true, but—"

"'Probably,' Joy?"

He was close, too close. She knew because of the way her skin, still sensitized from his touch, began to tingle and burn. It hadn't been that long ago that he had stroked and caressed her until she had nearly reached the ecstatic edge of climax. And now with his nearness, her already aroused senses began to clamor for him.

As nonchalantly as possible, she skirted the pool table until she was on the side opposite from him. When she sensed he was about to follow, she put up a hand. "Please don't. Stay there. I want us to talk about this. We need to settle it once and for all."

He stared at her for a long moment, then, exhaling a long breath, stripped off his jacket and tossed it aside. Slipping his hands into his slacks pocket, he said, "All right, Joy. I'm listening."

His focus on her was laser sharp, and just looking at him made her go weak in the knees and made heat quicken in her lower body. A woman would have to be crazy to walk away from him, she thought with one breath, and with the next, decided that was exactly what she had to do.

"I'm *still* listening, Joy."

"Okay, it's this. I've really enjoyed getting to know you, and I really like you as a friend, but—"

"Stop right there."

His voice boomed across the table with such force, she almost jumped.

"This sounds eerily similar to what you said earlier today to Ben, and *I* don't want to hear it."

"You're wrong," she said defensively. "It's not the same at all."

"Okay, then tell me where the difference is. A brush-off is a brush-off, Joy, any way you say it. If that's what you have in mind for me, you're going to have to come up with a new and different way to disguise it, because I'm not going to go away as easily as Ben did."

He was right, she thought with resignation. Her method had worked for all the others, but Caleb was different, and she had sensed it right from the start. The problem was, without her standard little talk to go by, she didn't quite know what to say. She tossed the cue ball down and watched as it rolled into a pocket and disappeared. "I don't expect you to understand this, but please try anyway. I told you I've never been interested in having a serious relationship."

"Who asked you for one?"

Pain pierced her heart. Before she had time to recover, he moved, coming around the pool table to her, his eyes burning with something dark and fierce.

Her chin came up. "It's true. No one has asked me for one, but I want you to know anyway—I won't, I can't go to bed with anyone unless I'm emotionally involved with that person."

Inexplicably he relaxed. He leaned back, resting a hip on the pool table, angling his body toward her. "Honey," he drawled, "I can promise making love with me will be *very* involving."

"You're not even *trying* to understand, Caleb."

He reached out, angling his hand along her jaw with his thumb around her chin. "You're wrong. I'm trying hard, maybe *too* damned hard. I'm trying so hard, I'm hurting. So now *you* try again, Joy.

Make me understand whatever it is you're trying to say. But I'm warning you, you only get one more try. After that, I'm taking you upstairs, and I promise you, together we'll make everything else irrelevant."

Heat washed over her as she imagined what it would be like to make love to him. Caleb's lovemaking would be intense, powerful, and fierce. She'd had a taste, a hint, back at the Malcolm estate. And she had to be honest. She had been seconds away from begging him to take her. All at once she realized that, right at this moment, she wanted him badly.

She turned her head away from him as tears of longing and helplessness welled in her eyes. Why couldn't she simply say yes, to him?

But even as she asked herself the question, she knew the answer. Years of ingrained conditioning was a powerful thing to overcome.

"People get hurt in serious relationships, Caleb. I've seen it time and again. I *hate* for people to get hurt. And I never want to hurt anyone. That's why I always break things off when I think a man is getting too serious."

With a finger beneath her chin, he brought her face around to him. "And you don't think that when you break off with a man it hurts him?"

She shook her head, dislodging his finger. "No, because I do it before he gets too involved."

"Honey," he drawled, "just looking at you is involving, don't you know that?"

"We're talking about two different things, Caleb."

"Yeah, I know. But I just want you to understand that you're not easy on a man, no matter how hard you try."

"What do you want me to do? Wear a sack over my head?"

"Now, that would be a crime."

"Then what?"

"I want you to give yourself to me, totally and completely."

"I can't do that."

"Your problem is not with me. It's with yourself."

Her eyes moistened again. "I can't think."

"Maybe that's better," he said, slowly undoing the black chiffon bow at her nape and drawing it from her hair.

"No, Caleb, it's not," she said desperately, knowing the situation was slipping from her grasp. Or maybe, she thought, she'd never had the situation in her grasp in the first place.

Using a hypnotically sensual rhythm, he combed his fingers through her hair, keeping his gaze on what he was doing rather than on her. "Has anyone ever hurt you, Joy?"

"No."

"Have you ever hurt anyone?"

She could feel herself warming inside, softening. "No. At least I hope not. I've tried not to."

His gaze returned to her face. "Then what if I promise not to let you hurt me?"

"It's not a promise you could make for sure."

"Do you think you're that irresistible?"

Uncertainty crept into her voice. "No, it's just that two people can start out with the best of intentions, but things seem to happen along the way, things over which neither has any control."

"It's all right," he said gently. "You *are* that irresistible. And it'll be easy not to let you hurt me. I'll just make you so happy, you'll never want to leave me."

She shook her head. "Caleb, that's not something you can know or control."

"Oh, yes, it is." He bent and pressed a kiss to her mouth. "And by the way, I'll also promise that I'll never hurt you."

"Caleb, people can and do make all the promises in the world to each other, but things happen."

"Not to us." He kissed her again.

"You haven't known me that long."

"I think I've known you forever, Joy."

He leaned toward her, grasped her by the shoulders, and kissed her. Instantly heat flamed up and ate its way through her until she was completely consumed by it, by him. *How terrifyingly easy*, she thought. *How amazingly wonderful*.

She should be used to his Caleb-kisses by now, she thought. The kind of kiss he gave so effortlessly, yet sapped everything out of her, leaving only the wanting. But through the haze of desire that was building around her, she sensed that this kiss was different from all the others. This kiss carried more purpose, more resolve, more power. This time she sensed he wasn't going to stop with kisses.

For a fraction of an instant he lifted his lips. "So think, Joy. Now's the time. Tell me. Do you want me?"

"Yes."

"Are you sure?"

"Yes. I want you more than I can say."

He tossed his glasses on the pool table, then kissed her, bringing his mouth down on hers again, plunging his tongue deep into her open mouth in hungry possession. A shiver raced through her, a shiver of fear of the unknown, a shiver of longing so strong, she was helpless against it. No matter what, she didn't want him to stop.

He felt the shiver and experienced a deep, pri-

mordial satisfaction. He was about to make her his.
And by all that was holy, he would keep her.

His hands dropped to the hem of her short black
skirt and pulled it up, dragging the tips of his fingers
up her silk-clad legs to the bare softness of her upper
thighs. He lingered there for a moment, exploring
higher, edging his fingers beneath her panties to the
waiting, hot dampness.

Surprise jolted through her, followed swiftly by
an indescribable pleasure. Somehow she knew his
touch would ease the ache deep inside her, even if it
was only momentary. Her nipples were hard, begging for attention, her breasts swelling. She felt
needy all over.

Only partly aware of what she was doing, she
unbuttoned her jacket, trying to alleviate some of
the tightness she was feeling. The slim, red strap of
the chemise, broken earlier, slid forward, bringing
the bodice of the chemise downward.

With a rough exclamation he gripped her hips
and lifted her onto the pool table, fitting her legs
around his waist.

He was hard and hurting, straining against the
fly of his trousers, but he didn't dare unzip his pants,
because he knew if he did, he wouldn't stop until he
had taken her right there on the pool table. At the
same time he wanted her too badly to allow anything
to block him from complete access to her. Tor-

mented almost beyond his endurance, he ground his pelvis against her. One impatient tug rent the delicate panties open, and then she was there for him, hot and moist and so inviting, he almost lost his mind.

He moved his mouth down her throat, fastened one hand firmly around a breast, the other he worked between them until he found what he was seeking, the hot core of her that he was determined he would know inside and out before the night was over.

She clung to his shoulders and locked her ankles behind his back. His fingers were creating a tension sweeter than anything she had ever known. She felt his fingers inside her, and the tension increased, coiling and twisting until she began to move, creating wondrous friction that sent exquisite fragments of heat all through her. "Caleb . . . ?"

He could take her right now, he thought feverishly. It would be so easy. Even his bones were shaking with the desire to do so. But some instinct held him back, telling him that the first time shouldn't be like this, here on the pool table, in haste and awkwardness.

With a growl he pulled his upper body away from her, though not enough that he dislodged her legs from around him. He smoothed her hair away from her face and looked deep into her eyes. "Hang on to me. We're going upstairs."

It wasn't exactly a question, yet it was, and the answer she gave wasn't exactly an answer, yet it was. "Please, Caleb . . ."

"Hell," he muttered. He shucked his T-shirt, then, wrapping his arms around her bottom, he lifted her. Her breasts pressed erotically against his bare chest. She was open to him and waiting. All he had to do was unzip his trousers.

He carried her up the stairs with the easy strength she had first sensed in him. His heart pounded against her breasts, matching the beat of her own heart. Her arms tightened their hold on his neck, and she put her lips against his mouth, not for a kiss, but just to be able to feel his breath, hot, sweet, and ragged, in her own mouth. She needed, *required*, this intimate connection to make it through the short space of time that would pass until they could achieve the ultimate connection.

Her mind had accepted the inevitable, and her whole body was shuddering with anticipation. She was going to make love to Caleb because she had to—there was no other choice for her. Later she would deal with the consequences. For there surely would be consequences.

In his bedroom he lowered her to his bed. As he looked down at her, she held up her arms to him. He shook his head, trying to clear his mind. There was something he knew, something he needed to remember, but nothing came to him. His mind was filled with the way she looked at this moment, with her long legs encased in filmy black stockings that stretched upward, ending on her upper thighs. The black skirt was bundled up around her hips, revealing the tantalizing torn edges of her red silk-and-lace panties and the top of the red chemise. One breast was bare, the nipple of the other breast was thrusting against the silk of her red chemise.

He hastily undressed, aware every second of her hungry eyes devouring him. Then, naked, he went down to her.

She immediately reached for him and set about exploring him. His body heat wrapped around her, his musky smell invaded her pores. Her hands eagerly skimmed over him, for the first time exploring his body, learning the muscles and flat planes of him, the texture of his skin and the tightly curling hair that spread across his chest and clustered at his groin. His full male length held particular fascination for her. Unable to resist, she took hold of him, stroking him from top to bottom, then encircling him with her hand.

After a few moments he caught her hands, bringing them together and holding them with one of his.

His chuckle held a raw, needy pain. "We're going to have to slow down, baby."

Her hips moved restively. "How? I'm going to come apart, Caleb."

He expelled a long, shuddering breath. "Not yet, not yet. . . . I want to undress you first. . . . I want to see you."

Slowly, with trembling hands, as if he were unwrapping a wondrous treasure, he slipped the clothes from her body.

There was something he should remember.

He pushed the hose down and flung them aside. They floated to the carpet, where they landed in a filmy drift. Her panties were next, and when they were free of her legs, he almost lost any remaining thread of control. There, at the juncture of her thighs, was a nest of pale-blond curls. Unable to resist, he buried his face in them and inhaled deeply. The scent of womanly desire exploded in his brain and wrecked his reason and sanity. He blew against her, then heard her moan, and his control shredded.

There was something he should remember.

"To hell with the rest of your clothes," he growled.

He raised up and reached to the side for the nightstand drawer where he kept protection. In seconds he had donned it and was parting her thighs.

He lowered himself onto her and at the same time began to enter her.

And then he remembered. "You're a virgin," he whispered, stunned by both the memory and the fact.

Joy barely heard him. She was caught up in a whirl of passion so powerful, she wasn't sure she'd ever escape it. When she again felt him between her thighs, she gave a little cry of relief. She blindly reached for him, clutching at his shoulders, mutely urging him to finish what he had started. The feel of him nudging against her gave only momentary relief, but the relief was fleeting, and then the hot hunger surged back even stronger.

She thrust her fingers up into his hair, brought his mouth down to hers, devouring him with feverish kisses, attempting to capture his tongue, trying in any way she knew how to get more relief.

A sheen of sweat broke out on his body, revealing the price he was paying for his care, but with an iron determination he proceeded slowly, entering her a little at a time, feeling her stretch around him. He would die, he thought, if he didn't bury his entire length in her soon. He had never felt such desire for a woman, never known such concern for her pleasure.

He tried to keep his pace slow. Lord, but he tried.

He did his best to keep her still, but she thrashed beneath him, crying out for him. And suddenly he could take no more. He lifted his hips and thrust deep and hard, burying himself completely in her. He felt her maidenhead tear, heard her take a sharp breath, and cursed himself even as an intense and mighty pleasure shot through him.

He tried to catch his breath, tried to ask her if she was all right, but then she was moving beneath him, and his last rational thought vanished.

He gripped her hips and began thrusting into her, his buttocks flexing, his powerful body straining. Making love to her was like nothing he had ever known before, and at the same time making love to her was exactly as he had known it would be. It defied description, it defied this world. She met him thrust for thrust, moving beneath him in perfect unison, and always demanding more. He complied.

She was his dream, his love. She was everything he had ever wanted without even knowing he had ever wanted. She was silk and fire, and most of all she was his, of that he was sure.

He was attuned to every nuance of her need, because it so exactly matched his. It was the most pleasure he'd ever known, the most hell. He had to wait, to wait. . . .

When the infinitesimal small quivers began deep within her, he felt them around him—and in his gut, in his heart, in his bones. They grew stronger, more powerful until her nails dug into his back, and she arched against him, her climax racking her.

The last vestige of his control broke. He held her tight, driving into her, savoring the way her muscles undulated around him, milking him until his own completion caught him unaware. It hit him with the force of a thunderous storm, convulsing his body, depleting his strength, destroying him, creating him.

Joy lay quietly beside Caleb, watching his chest rise and fall as his breathing slowly returned to normal. There had been nothing casual about his lovemaking, she reflected, nothing laid-back or easygoing.

What had happened? Lust—certainly. Passion—definitely. Ecstasy—absolutely.

She viewed herself differently now. She didn't know the woman who had just made love with Caleb. There hadn't been a particle of her being that hadn't been involved. She had held back nothing. After he had lifted her onto the pool table downstairs, there had been no point when she could have stopped and said, "No, wait." Making love to him had been more than a compulsion, it had been an absolute necessity.

She was astounded and dismayed by the violence of her own emotions that had been revealed during their lovemaking, so much so that she wasn't certain what she should do next.

He slipped an arm beneath her head and drew her against him. "Are you all right?"

Rather than trust herself to try to speak, she nodded.

He gently turned her head so that she was looking at him. "I'm sorry. I didn't know you were a virgin." *But he had known*, he realized, somewhat shaken. How?

She cleared her throat. "It doesn't matter."

"Did I hurt you?"

She put her hand on his chest and felt the rumble of his words. "It hurt just for a few seconds, and then . . . it didn't anymore." Then she had felt nothing but the most incredible pleasure she had ever known. Maybe, she thought, that pleasure was the reason people risked all for love. She understood so much more now. And she understood nothing.

The weight on the mattress shifted as he withdrew his arm and slipped from the bed. "Where are you going?" she asked, a hint of panic in her voice.

Panic? Why on earth did she feel so panic-stricken?

"I'll be right back."

He disappeared through a door. She looked after

him, inexplicably agitated by his absence and wanting to go after him. She heard water running, a toilet flushing, and then he was back, carrying a washcloth and climbing into bed beside her.

"This should feel good," he murmured, bending his head to press a light kiss to her lips and stroking the washcloth between her legs.

The warmth seeped into the tender tissue that had just been introduced to lovemaking in what had to be a world-class way, and incredibly his kiss stirred up a new heat in her blood. She had kissed him so many times, she wouldn't have believed she could ever want another kiss for the rest of her life. Yet she returned the kiss, holding nothing back.

He lifted his head and gazed down at her. "Does this feel good?" he asked, referring to the warm, moist heat of the washcloth.

"Everything you've done to me has felt good, Caleb."

A wry grin tugged at his mouth. "Maybe it'd be a good idea if, for now, you weren't so honest."

"Why?"

"Because I might forget that you're probably very tender."

As if to demonstrate, he pressed the washcloth up against her, and a new and different type of thrill raced through her.

She bit her bottom lip to stifle a moan. "Forget and do what?"

"Forget and make love to you again," he said, a bit bemused that she would have the question.

"Is that what's going to happen next?" She realized it was the question uppermost in her mind. "I could go home if you're tired."

"You're not going home, Joy." He resumed stroking her already sensitized tissue with the washcloth, and like magic heated excitement began to build once again.

"I've got to go home eventually," she said, beginning to fight for breath.

Holding her gaze, he slowly shook his head, and at the same time continued moving the washcloth back and forth. "No, you don't."

Urgency was rapidly reeling her into its grip. Her teeth captured her bottom lip, but this time the moan escaped from her. "Caleb, stop. . . . No, *don't* stop."

"Whatever you want."

His voice sounded deep and husky, but she couldn't see his expression because she'd closed her eyes. Between the washcloth and occasionally his fingers, he was creating sensation after exquisite sensation in her. Need was building upon need. Desire was threatening to spiral out of control. "I want *you*," she managed, and meant it with all her heart.

"You've got me," he whispered, his mouth very near her ear, his hot breath fanning into the delicate shell. Then his mouth closed over one of her nipples and tugged.

Passion picked her up and sent her hurling toward the peak. Crying out, she arched against his hand and reached out, wrapping her arms around his neck, increasing the pressure of his mouth on her breast, and she went off the edge, saying his name over and over.

"I love the way you climax," he whispered roughly. "In fact I want to see you do it again." And he drove into her.

SEVEN

Something was different. Joy knew it even before she opened her eyes. What could it be?

She was in a different bed than usual, Caleb's bed. But after all, a bed was only a bed. Besides since she'd been awake most of the night, making love to him, she'd had ample opportunity to get used to the bed.

Her body felt different, but that was to be expected. She had experienced so many new, astonishing, and wondrous sensations, she wouldn't be surprised to open her eyes and see that she had a whole new body. She *liked* the feelings.

But if it wasn't the bed or her body . . .

Caleb. That was it. He wasn't beside her. She was alone in the bed.

Each time she had awakened, she had felt him kissing her and touching her, a prelude to even more lovemaking. But now she couldn't feel him, his body, his heat. His body wasn't wrapped around hers, his limbs weren't entangled with hers.

Where was he?

Sheets twisting around her, her hair swinging forward in a mass of disheveled, glistening strands, she bolted upright, his name on her lips. She was thankful that she saw him before she actually called out for him.

He was leaning back in a cushioned chair at the foot of the bed, his bare feet propped on its edge. Wearing only a pair of jeans, he held a yellow legal pad in his lap and a pen in his hand.

"Good morning," he said with an easy smile. "I was hoping you'd sleep a little longer, but at the same time I was hoping you'd wake up."

She pushed her hair from her face, unaccountably out of sorts. "Which one, Caleb? It'd be a little tough for me to do both."

His smile broadened. "I suppose, but see, it's like this. I didn't give you a lot of time to rest during the night, so I know it'd be better if you could sleep for a few more hours. But the truth is, I was getting lonely without you and really hoping you'd wake up."

"Oh." In the past several days she had discovered that, like Pavlov's dog, she went weak at the sight of the same easygoing smile he was giving her now. But the smile faded into insignificance as she mentally reviewed the arsenal of new weapons he now possessed to use against her, weapons of seduction and passion that scared her out of her mind, scared her because she had no strength to use against them, scared her because she had no urge to fight against them.

She needed a defensive tactic, if only temporarily. She nodded toward the yellow pad. "What are you doing?"

He cast a dismissive glance at the notepad. "Working on a problem."

"For your business?"

"Uh-huh."

After a night of startling intimacy, the impersonal note of the conversation was a pitifully weak tactic, but for the moment it was all she had.

Almost from the first moment she had met Caleb, she had been thrown off balance. But any sort of equilibrium that might have remained before last night was now a thing of the past. Her world and her ideas had been bent, skewed, and generally damaged beyond recognition. Somehow, some way, she had to regroup. "Your work is obviously very important to you."

"It always has been." He tossed the legal pad aside and leaned forward, an expression of concern on his face. "How are you feeling? Can I get you anything?"

"I'm fine." She couldn't decide which was worse, his easygoing smile or his earnest, concerned expression. She finally decided that *all* his expressions were equally devastating. "I'm fine. What time is it?"

Without looking at his watch, he said, "There's time."

Her forehead pleated, as she wondered, not for the first time, if she had missed something. "Time for what?"

"For anything we want."

She barely managed to resist the temptation to smile and hold out her arms to him. "Caleb, I really need to know what time it is. Grace's shop is my responsibility."

He shifted from the chair to a spot on the bed beside her. "Exactly when is this sister of yours coming home?"

"Soon."

"It can't be too soon for me."

"Why? Once she's home, I'll go back to my own shop. I'll still have responsibilities. I won't be able to be late."

"But you must have left your shop in someone's hands whom you trust enough to enable you to work full-time at Grace's shop. Right?"

She nodded slowly, wondering where he was going with his question. "Yes."

"And since you've done it this long, I was hoping maybe you could do it a little longer. I'd like us to take off somewhere together for a holiday."

"A holi—" Panic surged through her, momentarily taking her by surprise. After the night's intimacy it was only natural for him to ask her to go away with him. Under the circumstances his invitation wasn't out of line. Her panic definitely was however, and she had to get it under control. "I can't do that."

"Why?"

"I just can't, that's all." It was hard for her to put into words something that frightened her so much. She reached for his wrist and took a quick look at his watch. "Oh, Lord, it's after eight. I have to go." She pushed the sheets away from her, remembered she was naked, then jerked them back against her again. "Do you have a robe? Have you seen my clothes? Is there any coffee?"

"There's coffee. We'll find your clothes—"

She snapped her fingers. "Oh, wait, I don't have a car. You're going to have to take me home. No, wait, I could call a cab. Where's the phone?"

He pressed a soft kiss to her lips, lengthening the kiss until he felt her subside against him. Lifting his head, he smoothed her hair back from her face. "Do you normally wake up this confused and frantic?"

She straightened away from him. "I'm not confused *or* frantic. I'm just not in a house I'm familiar with, and my mind started working all at once. Do you have a robe I could borrow?"

"Sure. Somewhere." He paused, his expression slightly quizzical. "If you were my bathrobe, where do you think you'd be?"

"Try the back of your bathroom door."

She sighed as she watched him walk away. The man was astounding. He might not pay attention to relatively simple matters such as where he kept his bathrobe, but the same couldn't be said for his attitude toward her. The night that had just passed was a prime example of that. He had learned her body well, as she had his.

In fact she had paid so much attention to Caleb, she hadn't even noticed her surroundings. But now she glanced around her, curiosity mixing with a fervent desire to get her mind off his effect on her. His bed, the bed on which they had made love practically the whole night through, consisted of nothing more than a king-sized mattress and box-spring set resting atop a platform. Across the room a multicomponent, state-of-the-art stereo system dominated. Two tall, multidrawer mahogany chests stood against another wall. Two laptop computers and one desk-top computer resided on a long table.

And everywhere there were books and piles of yellow legal pads.

Caleb returned, robe in hand. "You were right. How'd you know it would be there?"

"Didn't you tell me you have a housekeeper?"

He nodded. "Yes."

"It makes sense that she would hang it where she thought you'd find it. Besides that's where most people hang their robes." Her tone was wry. "And by the way, your keys are over there on the desk by the computer."

"Oh, good, then I can take you home."

"Caleb, about this bedroom . . . ?"

"What about it?"

"Well, it's just that it's not decorated like the downstairs. It doesn't seem as finished."

"It's not decorated at all. I told Daisy to hold off on it until I figured out what I wanted in here. That was about five years ago."

"She did the decorating downstairs?"

"Yeah, she's good at that sort of thing."

"Does she do it professionally?"

"No, she does it for fun and whenever she's in the mood. But doing this house was no challenge for her. She just took a lot of things I like and put them together."

"How nice to have someone who knows you that well."

His eyes twinkled with knowing amusement. "You should know. You have Grace."

"That's hardly the same thing. It's natural that Grace and I are close."

"Right. And it's just as natural that Daisy and I are close."

She wasn't going to win this argument, she thought, irritated with herself, nor probably would she ever understand the connection between Caleb and his cousin.

In some ways the night had brought amazing changes. She and Caleb had shared an intimacy she still found shattering. Then again, nothing had changed. She foresaw disaster if she stayed with Caleb much longer. Yet she wasn't willing to leave him. Not yet.

She snatched the robe from him, stood, and shrugged into it, then began searching for her clothes.

Very gently he closed his hand around her upper arm and stilled her. "Stop worrying, Joy."

"How did you know—?" Silly question, she thought. He seemed to know everything about her.

He watched the varying expressions cross her face, and his heart surged with love. He was very much in love with her. Very much. And his love for her had happened so easily and naturally, it was almost as if the love had always been in him. "It's going to be all right, Joy. You, me, us. We're going to be okay."

"I know."

His lips twisted with wry humor. "No, you don't, and nothing I say right now is going to make you feel any better. In fact if I said the words I truly wanted to say, I'd only make you feel worse."

She gave a shaky laugh. "That's what I like about you, Caleb. You always make so much sense."

"Okay, how about this: There are some men who know the words that will make a woman feel better and say them whether they mean them or not. I know the words, but I've never said them. I've never wanted to until now."

She shook her head, panic again rising in her. "Look, Caleb, you don't have to say a word. I don't need it. I'm an adult. I wouldn't have spent the night in your bed if I hadn't wanted to."

With a thumb beneath her chin he lifted her face to his. "It was beyond anything I could ever have imagined."

"*Don't.*" She jerked away from him. "I told you. I don't need to hear any of that stuff."

"Then tell me what you need."

She tried for another laugh, but this time failed. "I'm probably going to need a giant-sized Band-Aid for all my hurts before this is over."

"I told you I wasn't going to hurt you, Joy, and I meant it."

"And I told you you weren't going to hurt me."

Glancing around for her panties, she had a vague recollection of them being torn and unwearable. She scooped up her skirt, but held it against her for a moment as she looked at him. "I'm going to do my best not to be hurt and not to hurt you, but as I said before, there just aren't any guarantees. If I were smart, I'd leave here this morning and not come back."

"I hope I heard a *but* there."

She shrugged, and focused her eyes at the base of his throat. She had the courage to be honest, but not enough to meet his eyes. "There is. There's a very big one."

"And what's that?"

"I don't feel very smart at the moment. I don't think I could just go away and not come back. I mean, all you have to do is look at me and—"

"And what?"

She peered upward through her lashes at him. "And I practically go to pieces, all right?"

"No," he murmured roughly, closing the distance between them. "If you're going to go to pieces, I want it to be in my arms." He slipped his hands inside the robe to her waistline and pulled her against him so that her naked breasts were crushed against his broad, muscled chest. "And I want to be kissing you." He caught her mouth in a hot, hard kiss that fired her insides and rekindled her desire.

Her hands gripped his shoulders as he moved her backward, then down, down onto the bed. She closed her eyes, aching from her head to her toes with need for him.

"And when you go to pieces," he muttered, "I want to be inside you."

He surged into her, hard and powerful, filling her, and she knew she'd been waiting for that exact moment since she had awakened, alone and without him.

And then, almost before she knew it, she was going to pieces. But it was all right, because she was in his arms, and he was kissing her, and he was inside her, exactly where she wanted him to be.

The phone was ringing when Joy raced into Grace's house sometime later. Deciding to let the answering machine pick up the call, she headed for the bedroom and a change of clothes. But when she heard the concerned sound of her sister's voice, she had no choice but to snatch up the phone. "Hi, Grace. It's me."

"Joy, where have you been? I called you last night, but you didn't answer."

"I was at the auction," she said, thinking fast. "Remember?"

"I remember, but it shouldn't have gone on as late as midnight, which is when I called."

"I was with Caleb," she said, hoping to divert Grace.

"Caleb?"

"Caleb McClintock. He's the man I told you could tell us apart."

"Oh, right. The weird one. What were you doing with him?"

What *hadn't* she done with him, would be a better question and most definitely an easier question to answer. "He was my date for the evening."

"Oh . . ."

She and Grace had always been able to communicate, even before they had been able to talk. And now her instinct was to tell her sister everything. Under normal circumstances she would have, but the things that were happening in her life had thrown her completely off balance. It would be hard, if not impossible for her to find the words to convey what she was feeling. She wasn't sure she could figure it out herself, and until she did, she didn't want to worry Grace. "Everything went fine at the auction. I think I was able to get everything you wanted."

"You *think*?"

"Right, well, you know how last-minute snags can crop up."

"No, actually, I don't. You either bid and get it or you don't."

Joy grimaced. "Right. That's what I just said. So how's it going up there?"

"Better and better," Grace said, excitement growing in her voice. "Joy, you wouldn't believe my finds. This is going to put my shop on the map."

"That's great. I couldn't be happier for you. Listen, sweetie, I've got to go. If I don't hurry, I'm going to be late opening the shop."

"I know. You should already be there. What's wrong? Why are you running so late?"

She had never lied to Grace in her life, but in certain cases, when it was for Grace's own good, she had omitted certain pertinent facts. This was the time to omit facts. "No particular reason. It's just one of those mornings. Listen, have a good day and I'll talk to you soon. 'Bye."

In the end Joy was only twenty minutes late to the shop and, considering how much later Caleb had wanted to make her, she congratulated herself for doing as well as she had. But she'd no sooner turned on all the lights and tuned the stereo to Grace's favorite classical station when Bertrand walked in, carrying a silver tray and wearing a frown on his face.

"My dear, I've been most concerned about you."

She really wasn't up to dealing with Bertrand this morning, she thought, mentally groaning. "Have you? Why?"

His eyebrows shot up. "Well, I would say it's rather obvious. You were out last night when you shouldn't have been. You left early, which I assumed meant you had taken a turn for the worst. And then you arrive late to the shop this morning. I was ready to begin calling the hospitals."

The genuine concern on his face stopped the flip remark she had been about to make. Bertrand had no compunction when it came to professional dirty tricks, but neither Grace nor she had ever for a moment believed he wished Grace personal ill. He had just never been able to understand that Grace took the business every bit as seriously as he did. "I'm sorry you were concerned, Bertrand, but I'm fine, really I am. I ran a few errands on my way here, and they took me longer than I had expected. That's all." She would never lie to Grace, but she didn't mind telling Bertrand a few white fibs.

Bertrand rewarded her white fibs with a more pronounced frown. "Errands?"

"Really," she said. "My cold is *much* better. I think I just needed a good night's sleep." She *still* needed a good night's sleep, she reflected wryly.

"Errands or not," he said, scrutinizing her, it's simply not like you to be late, my dear, and the fact of the matter is, you don't look well. You really don't. I wish you'd consult my physician."

First chance she got, she thought determinedly, she was going to put on more blusher. "I'm really feeling much better, but I'll make you a deal. If I start to feel worse, I promise I'll go to a doctor." She nodded toward the napkin-covered tray. "What do you have there?"

"Tea and scones. I thought it might be just the thing for you. I brewed the tea myself, and the scones were baked fresh this morning by my house-keeper. I always say there's nothing like a spot of tea to make a body feel better."

"That's very considerate of you, Bertrand," she said, and meant it. She indicated a clear space on her desk. "Join me."

"Thank you. I'd like that." He placed the tray on her desk, settled his elegant frame into a chair, whisked off the napkin, and poured out the tea. "So what happened last night? Did you in fact take a turn for the worse?"

"Uh . . . not exactly, but I suppose you could say that I wasn't feeling quite myself. How did the auction go? Did you get everything you wanted?"

"Not quite everything." His tone expressed dis-pleasure.

He must not have been able to get the bed, Joy thought, hard pressed not to chuckle aloud. She dropped down in the chair behind the desk. "I'm sorry."

He dismissed her sympathy with a wave of his hand. "It doesn't matter. I was able to acquire several splendid pieces. Too bad you weren't able to get anything at all."

"Ummm." Since she couldn't be specific about the pieces she'd gotten until she talked to Daisy, she decided not to say anything on the subject. She spread liberal portions of raspberry jam across a scone and bit into it.

Bertrand stared hard at her. "I thought you didn't care for raspberry jam. I brought the apricot jam for you."

Too late she remembered that Grace didn't like raspberries. She picked up a knife and hurriedly scraped off the jam. "How funny," she said wryly. "I guess my cold has affected my taste buds. I didn't even notice."

Bertrand settled back in his chair. "Your taste buds *and* apparently your eyesight. One jam is red, the other gold."

She gave him a sweet smile and bit into the scone now spread with apricot jam.

Bertrand took a sip of his tea. "What a fascinating fellow, your Mr. McClintock. How ever did you meet him?"

"First of all, he's not *my* Mr. McClintock," she said dryly. "And as for how I met him, I just sort of ran into him."

"How fortuitous for you, my dear."

"You think so?" she asked with deliberate innocence.

"Definitely. His reclusive nature makes him a very desirable prey."

"*Prey*." She repeated the word, but didn't need a moment's thought to decide it didn't fit Caleb at all. *Predator*, but not *prey*.

Bertrand waved his ebony cigarette holder with its unlit cigarette in the air and stood. "You know what I mean. At any rate I'd better be off. I'm sure it will be a busy morning." He paused by the Federal satinwood sewing table that he had commented on before. "By the way, if I were you, I'd put this in your back room for a while."

"What ever for?"

"I told you before." He shrugged. "Whatever you paid for it, you paid too much. Anyway, it's just a thought."

"Wait. What about the tea tray?"

"Keep it for now and finish off the tea. I'll pop over late to pick it up."

Wonderful, she thought. Just what she didn't

need, another encounter with Bertrand. He was hard enough for her to handle under normal circumstances, but today her mind wasn't totally on the job at hand. Caleb . . . her mind was on Caleb.

The florist arrived about an hour later, bringing a beautiful mixed bouquet and a card that said, *To Grace: I hope you're feeling better. Think you'll be well by the weekend? Take care of yourself. I'll call soon. Jeremy.*

Grace's wannabe boyfriends all seemed very nice, but they weren't amazing and wonderful like . . . like Caleb. And whoever Grace fell in love with, Joy wanted that love to last forever, instead of the short time she and Caleb would be together.

A little after noon the bells tinkled, and Joy turned to see a couple walk in. The woman's hair was enormous and, Joy judged, had to weigh at least one-third of the woman's total body weight. The man, however, was bald.

"Good afternoon," she said, greeting them with a professional smile of which Grace would have been proud.

The man slapped down a sales receipt on her desk. "We want our money back."

She instinctively stiffened. "May I ask why?"

"Because the Chippendale secretaire you sold us is a fake."

Shaking her head firmly, she picked up the sales

receipt and glanced at the name there. "It couldn't be, Mr. and Mrs. Morrison."

"I assure you it is. We had an independent appraisal done for insurances purposes, and the piece has been declared a fraud. According to the appraiser, it was the drawers that gave it away. The dovetails were too small and too uniform to have been handmade. It was something we never would have thought to look at. All we wanted was a showpiece."

She glanced again at the receipt and nearly blanched at the twenty-thousand-dollar price. For the first time in her life she wished she knew more about antiques. But Grace was the one who had taken to the subject as if she'd been born to it, whereas she had taken an interest in the clothing business. "If you're unhappy with the piece—"

The wife spoke up. "I loved it, and it looked perfect in our foyer, but you can't expect us to pay the price we did for a fake."

This didn't make sense, Joy thought uneasily. First Mrs. Emerson yesterday, and now the Morrisons. "If it is a fake, and mind you I'm saying *if*, then a terrible mistake has been made, and I can promise you I will get to the bottom of it. In the meantime I'll have it picked up first thing in the morning, and your money returned immediately. My reputation is my business, and I take this very seriously."

"As well you should," Mr. Morrison said. "We will be expecting our check."

Joy sank into her desk chair and shut her eyes. When she opened her eyes, Caleb was standing there. As usual with him she hadn't heard the bells.

"How long have you been standing there?"

"Long enough. Now will you tell me what's going on and why you're pretending to be your sister?"

She pushed back her hair. "I don't know what's going on. Two customers have said furniture that Grace sold them is fake. Grace is very, very good at what she does, and she simply wouldn't sell something that wasn't genuine."

"Not even if it meant a quick profit?" The look she gave him would have melted stone, but he received it with equanimity. "I had to ask."

"The answer is no. No way, no how."

"Then tell me what you're doing pretending to be her."

She shrugged impatiently. "One thing's got nothing to do with the other."

"Maybe not, but tell me anyway."

She sighed, knowing she was going to tell him. This man had managed to get around most of her barriers in an incredibly short period of time. If she thought about it too long, she reflected half humorously, she might decide it was her patriotic duty to turn him over to the proper authorities as a national security risk. If he could so easily get around her barriers, there was no telling what he could do to the national defense system.

"It has to do with Bertrand." She waved her hand toward the front windows, indicating his shop across the street. As I told you, he's a fierce competitor. When Grace first opened her shop, he saw her as a dilettante, a young woman who had nothing more than money and connections going for her on a professional level. And he's never given up the idea or the hope that Grace is going to grow bored with the antiques business eventually and move on to some other little hobby, and every once in a while he does something to hasten her departure."

"Like what?"

"Oh, like bidding up the price of something he knew Grace wanted, then dropping out. Or like seeing that she receives the wrong date for an estate sale, or telling the postman he'll make sure she gets her mail and then conveniently forgetting to deliver it until after some important event." She grinned. "But then, she's gotten her own back." Her grin widened. "Once she switched directions to a sale." Her smile faded, and she rubbed her forehead. "Of course *I* did that. Grace isn't quite that underhanded. At any rate Grace has spent a great deal of time cultivating contacts, all on the up and up. And through one of these contacts she received word about an estate sale in upstate New York. Because of all the time she spent cultivating this particular contact, she was notified first and was ultimately given an exclusive. Of course she didn't want Bertrand to know about it. We're not just talking about one or two showcase pieces like we saw last night. This is a veritable treasure trove, and she's in the process of sinking a hell of a lot of her capital in it, but it will absolutely *make* her store. Bertrand will *have* to accept her as an equal after this, but we just want to keep it all quiet until it is a *fait accompli*."

The doorbell tinkled, and Daisy breezed in, managing to look beautiful and fashionable in jeans, a T-shirt, and an armful of gold bracelets. "I have the sales receipts for the pieces I managed to get for you last night." She paused by the sewing table. "You know, there's something odd about this table."

EIGHT

Joy's nerves tightened. "Why do you say that?"

"I don't know. Maybe it's nothing, but I didn't think your sister dealt in reproductions."

"She doesn't."

"No?" After a moment's further examination Daisy shrugged and continued on to the desk where Joy and Caleb were.

Involuntarily Joy turned to Caleb, instinctively looking for help in understanding.

"I told you Daisy is good at decorating," he said, "and she's picked up some knowledge here and there about furniture over the years. It's just one of the things she's good at."

Daisy chuckled, drawing Joy's gaze. "Jack-of-all-trades, master of none, that's me."

"But you think there's something wrong with the table?"

Daisy made a vague gesture. "It's probably nothing."

"Yeah, but if it wasn't probably nothing, what would it be?"

"I don't know. It just doesn't look quite . . . *authentic* to me. Just an impression. I'm certainly no expert. But you might want to check it out. Anyway"—she wiggled a batch of sales receipts in the air—"I got your sister everything on her shopping list but one thing, and Bertrand Partington outbid me on it."

Not authentic. Joy took the receipts and glanced through them, a frown pleating her forehead. *Not authentic.* That was impossible. Grace simply didn't make mistakes like that. "Thanks, Daisy, I appreciate it."

"No problem."

"I'll total these receipts and write you a check right away."

"That'll be fine." Daisy smiled at her cousin. "I got what you wanted too. They've already been delivered, and I had the one item set up for you. You have to decide where you want the other."

Caleb smiled. "Thanks, sugar."

"It was fun. That Mr. Partington nearly turned purple when the gavel came down on my bid."

He grinned, his face alight with tenderness and love. "You're so *bad*."

She laughed again, then lightly poked him in the chest with a forefinger. "Yeah, I know, but then, so are you. Margie says she and the crew are having a tougher time than usual. It seems when you deign to come into the office these days, you don't stay long and leave a lot of loose ends dangling."

"They'll cope. They always do."

"Beautifully," she agreed, and glanced at the leather-banded watch on her wrist. "I'd better go. I'm catching a plane out of here in a couple of hours. I'm going back down to Austin for a few days. There's a couple of parties I want to catch."

"Don't forget to call and check in with me, okay?"

"You know I won't." She glanced at Joy. "The auction pieces will be delivered tomorrow. Oh, and just give my check to Caleb. He'll take care of it for me."

Joy nodded, struggling to remain calm in the face of so much she didn't understand. Daisy, Bertrand, Caleb. . . . What should have been a relatively simple week spent pretending to be her sister was rapidly turning into a complex, complicated puzzle. "Thanks again."

"Sure. I was glad to help." Daisy put her slender arms around Caleb in a tight hug and whispered something in his ear. He whispered back, and then they kissed each other lightly on the lips.

In many ways Joy felt like an interloper, viewing a relationship closed to all outsiders. She wasn't jealous, she told herself firmly, just curious. And in reality she didn't even have a right to be curious.

Daisy drew away from him and gave Joy a smile. "See you around."

Joy lifted a hand in farewell. When she looked back at Caleb, she found him watching her with an unnerving perceptiveness. It wasn't right, she thought resentfully, that he should understand so much while she understood so little. Without warning him what she was going to do, she pulled his glasses from his face and took them with her to the Regency sideboard where the linen napkins were kept. With an agitated energy uncalled for by the task, she cleaned his glasses.

He watched her for a moment, then strolled over to her, took the glasses from her, and slipped them back on. "Okay, listen, Joy. All I'm going to say for now is that neither Daisy nor I had a great childhood with the regulation two parents and the one-point-five dogs."

"First of all, Caleb, what makes you think your relationship with Daisy matters to me? And second of all, that's supposed to be two-point-five *kids*, not dogs."

"Whatever, we didn't have it."

"Grace and I didn't either, but we had great

grandparents." A feeling of weariness washed over her. She needed sleep. She needed her own life back. She needed to flirt, to have a good time without having to worry about ties that bind or desires that tore through her and made her want to cling. . . .

"And you had each other."

"And we had each other," she acknowledged.

"Just like Daisy and me, except we didn't have great grandparents. We only had each other."

She sighed. She knew what it was like to be so close to a person that there were things only the two of you shared, and he was saying that his and Daisy's relationship was like what she and Grace had shared all their life. Maybe she'd get a further explanation, maybe she wouldn't, but it didn't matter. She understood now, whether she wanted to or not. She rubbed an ache near her temple.

"You're tired," Caleb said.

Coming from him, the comment struck her as funny, and she chuckled. "Well, I wonder why."

"Yeah, well. . . . Let me take you home." His grin was sheepish and almost irresistible.

Almost. She shook her head. "I can't leave yet. There's something going on here with Grace's business, and I've got to figure it out."

"Are you talking about the two pieces of furniture that have been returned?"

"Plus the sewing table. Both Bertrand and Daisy have said something about it."

He stroked the back of his hand along her cheek in a gentle caress. "You know, don't you, that it could be just some gigantic coincidence."

"It could be, but I just don't know if I can risk leaving it at that."

"Why not? Why not let the matter ride? Grace will be home soon, and when she does get back, she can look into it."

"Like I said, I don't know if I can risk it. We're talking about my sister's reputation here. A lot is riding on what she's doing now. But it will all mean nothing if she comes home and her reputation has been destroyed. I just have this feeling that I need to do something to stop this before it gets out of hand. The problem is I don't know where to start."

He reached for her, drawing her against him. "You're not going to be able to start anywhere if you don't get some sleep. Come home with me."

She allowed herself to rest against him. She knew she couldn't stay within the circle of his arms indefinitely, of course, no matter how strong the temptation. She had problems to deal with, two to be exact. The first being whatever was happening in Grace's business, and the second being Caleb.

But she was tired, too tired even to think straight. And Caleb offered solace. He had already begun to weave himself into the fabric of her life, so thoroughly that she was already admitting to herself that she would have trouble keeping away from him for long. There would come a time, and soon, when she would have to undertake the task of unraveling him from her life. But somehow she didn't think tonight was the time. "Will I get any rest?"

His smile was compelling. "Sooner or later."

"The *bed*!" Joy walked slowly into Caleb's bedroom, her mouth slightly agape as she gazed at the bed, the same massive four-poster canopied and draped bed in which they had nearly made love last night at the Malcolm estate.

"It looks right in here, doesn't it?" Caleb said, satisfaction in his voice.

"It looks *great*, but how—?"

He turned to her. "You know, it's an interesting thing. Daisy showed me the auction catalog before we went, and I picked out two items before I ever saw them. The bed and one other."

"Which one other?" she asked, although one particular object flashed into her mind.

"The chandelier."

A strange sensation trickled down her spine as he mentioned the object that she had been thinking of. "The Louis XV chandelier that I looked at?"

He nodded. "The one I thought we had danced under. Remember? You were golden that night in yards of silk and lace, and I held you as tight as I dared with all those people surrounding us."

Light showering over them. Laughter. Music. The swish of silk. The feel of Caleb's hard thighs against hers.

Deeply shaken by the disconcerting snippets of memory that flashed in spurts of blinding light in her head, she cleared her throat. "I remember you saying that, but . . ."

"There was something about the chandelier's picture in the catalog that appealed to me, just like the picture of the bed did. But I didn't get a sense that you and I had danced beneath the chandelier or made love in the bed until I actually saw the pieces."

"You're making this up, Caleb." She had somehow managed to convince herself she could handle a love affair with him, but she definitely couldn't handle ties to him that stretched through other lives. It would be too bizarre, too unfathomable, too *unalterable*. "It's incredibly strange."

"You think this makes sense to me? Remember when I told you that I haven't been able to decide what I wanted in here for the last five years? The minute I saw the bed in the catalog, I knew it belonged here. The only thing I'm going to change is the gold spread and draperies. Red seems right to me. You were wearing the color the day we met, and

I get the feeling I've seen the bed before, swathed in a beautiful garnet color."

Garnet. Another life in which she had loved Caleb. No, she couldn't accept loving him in *this* life, must less in another. "Where are you going to put the chandelier?"

"Somewhere where we can dance beneath it."

No. No. *No.* She passed a hand across her eyes. "You know, I am really tired."

"Believe it or not, I am too."

With hands that were both gentle and sure on her body, he undressed her while she stood quietly, obediently, offering no resistance. Then after stripping out of his own clothes, he drew her into the bed with him, tugged the covers up over them, pulled the draperies closed around them, and snuggled her against him. Contentment and peace washed over Joy, and she drifted off to sleep.

Sometime in the night she awakened, rested and free of concern, and she reached out for Caleb. She found him very close, awake and watching her.

"We sleep well in this bed, don't we?"

"Yes, at least we did tonight."

He smoothed her hair back from her face. "And I bet we're going to make spectacular love in it."

Her nerves and doubts temporarily soothed by sleep, she smiled softly. "Is that a statement of intent?"

He idly skimmed his hand over her stomach. "I said I *bet* we're going to make spectacular love, but I shouldn't have. I should have said I *know* we will, because somehow I do." He leaned over and kissed her, a butterfly kiss made out of lightness and air, but it sent a flash of heat deep into her belly.

She put a hand on his shoulder and pushed until he straightened away. "Listen, Caleb," she said, her tone husky but serious, "you've got to believe me. That day we met and I said the wagon train ran over you in our previous life, I didn't really mean it."

"Then why did you say it?" His expression was serious.

"I don't know. You startled me because I thought you were about to get run over, and the words just came out."

"Had you ever said anything like that before?"

"Well . . . no, not exactly."

"Anything *close* to it?"

"No."

His expression relaxed. "So, tell me, did you grieve for me after the wagon train ran over me?"

"Caleb!" The exclamation of exasperation sounded startlingly loud. Up to that point both of them had been speaking in hushed tones.

"Look, I'm not sure myself about this. Except . . . I can't stop myself from wondering. I mean, the experience so traumatized you, you said that you swore you'd never let it happen again. And by the way"—light twinkled in his eyes as he took her hand from his shoulder and brought her palm to his mouth for a warm kiss—"I have to say you've done a great job ever since. Not *one* wagon train has run over me."

She groaned in frustration. "You're not listening to me."

He lowered his head and nuzzled his lips to the sensitive indentation behind her ear. "I always listen to you, Joy. It's become one of the greatest pleasures of my life."

His words combined with the feel of his lips threatened to undo her resolve, but this particular argument was important to her. She needed to get him off the subject of their having been together in other lives. It was not only ridiculous, it was completely unsettling to her. And since she had indeed been the one to bring it up in the first place, though she still had no idea why she had, she felt the responsibility of laying the subject to rest. "Okay, if you always listen to me, then hear me now. It *never* happened, Caleb."

All lightness left his voice, and planting his elbows on either side of her for support, he raised up. "Maybe it didn't, but maybe it did."

"It didn't."

"Yeah, but let's just say it did. As I said, you must have been devastated—"

"Traumatized. You said traumatized."

"In this case is there a difference?"

She made a sound of annoyance and turned her head along the pillow in the opposite direction. "What does it matter? It's foolish even to pursue it."

"I honestly don't know why this is important to me or why I'm feeling the things I'm feeling. But hang in here and follow along on this with me. Now, I think we can both agree that you were either severely traumatized or devastated. Right?"

Her voice held patience that was stretched dangerously thin. "Most people would be if they witnessed someone being run over by a wagon train."

"Right, and that thought leads beautifully into my next question." With a hand against her chin he turned her head back. "Do you think it was just normal trauma?" She opened her mouth to speak, but he stopped her. "Wait. Think about this. I mean, you said that you vowed you would never let it happen again. That implies a little more than normal trauma, don't you think?"

"Caleb, you are *so* weird."

"Just tell me—do you think you grieved for me?"

She looked at him. On the other side of the bed hangings a lamp had been left burning. Its light filtered through the silk hangings and created a haze of pale-golden light that seemed to surround him. Grieve for him? If she ever lost him, under any circumstances, she knew without a doubt that she would never get over him. *Until she found him again.*

As the implication of her thoughts soaked into her, fear began to choke her. No, it *couldn't* be true. She *refused* to let it be true.

She pushed against him until he rolled away, and she sat up in a wild panic, her hair swinging forward, sweat breaking out on her forehead, her heart beating wildly.

"Joy, what's wrong?" he asked, coming up beside her. "Tell me!"

"I've got to go home." She shook her head as if the action would help her straighten her thoughts out. "I mean, to Grace's home."

He shifted forward and combed her hair away from her face with his fingers. "It's the middle of the night. I've never liked the idea of you out at this time of night."

Her eyes widened. "Excuse me?"

Realizing what he had said, he briefly closed his eyes. When he reopened them, he said, "I *don't* like the idea."

"Tough," she said clearly, distinctly.

"If you insist on going, then I'm coming with you."

"Do you really think you can find your car keys?"

"I can always find things and people that are truly important to me."

She wasn't going to get away from him, she realized, then quickly amended her thought. *Not tonight at any rate*. Basically because she didn't want to. The idea of him dropping her off at Grace's, of her entering Grace's pretty bedroom and climbing alone into her bed, left her absolutely cold.

"I'll stay," she said, and lay back down. Her hair clouded over the pillow like a golden mist.

"There are only a few more hours until dawn," he murmured, gazing down at her.

She recognized the hunger in his gaze and shut her eyes, trying to seal herself away from him and the need he engendered in her. He watched her for a moment longer, she knew because she could feel the force of his gaze on her skin. If she gave in and opened her eyes, she knew they would end up making love.

But then there was movement as he lay down. Surprisingly he left space between them so that he wasn't touching her. But she could hear each breath he took and feel the heat of his body as it radiated out from him. She could even feel his desire for her as if it were a tangible thing.

She opened her eyes and gazed up at the underside of the bed's golden-silk canopy.

Red. She saw red instead of gold! She squeezed her eyes shut, then opened them again. *Gold. Thank heavens*, she thought, breathing a silent sigh of relief.

She didn't believe in past lives, didn't want to, *especially* when those other lives involved Caleb. To be linked by past lives implied more than permanence, it implied something that was eternal, something unable to be broken apart.

She knew no such thing existed. Sure, there were couples, like her grandparents who had managed to stay together for a longer-than-average period of time, but they were rare, an anomaly in the natural order of things. Besides, she knew why they had stayed together. When she and Grace had been small, her mother had left her father, the act destroying him in every way. Her grandparents had had no choice but to stay together to raise her and Grace.

Witnessing the events, her own tender heart had been crushed, and she vowed she would never hurt anyone the way her mother had hurt her father. Her desertion had left him visibly ravaged, and he had quickly lost the will to live, killing himself in the attic one bright spring day while his daughters played downstairs.

She had learned that it always paid to keep a door open in a relationship. She had learned it paid to avoid emotional entanglements.

She turned her head along the pillow to look at Caleb. His eyes were closed, but she knew he wasn't asleep. For someone so laid-back he could produce an enormous amount of electricity, even when he was lying still—electricity and magnetism.

He was doing nothing, but she could still feel herself wanting to reach out to him, to touch him, to kiss him, to allow herself to get swallowed up by the fire of their mutual desire.

She could do without him of course. It wasn't as if she was becoming addicted to him. Besides, even if she was, she could break the addiction when the time came. She had the strength and she certainly had the motivation.

Was there a rehab program to help rid her of her addiction to Caleb, she wondered, forcing her gaze away from him to the canopy above her.

What a magnificent, quixotic, wonderful bed. She couldn't help but love it. *Red brocade*. Yes, she could almost see it. Heavy and dense, the deep red of a garnet. It would keep the cold out and the heat of their desire in. It would also make her feel secure, as if the draperies were keeping the world at bay, as it was now.

"Caleb?" His name was a whisper on her lips, a wish.

"Ummm?"

"You knew I was a virgin before you . . ." Afraid to go on, she drew in a soft breath.

"Yes."

She looked over at him. "How?"

In the golden light his eyes looked very blue. "I don't know. Just a feeling I had, but at that instant it was very strong and impossible to ignore."

"A feeling that I was a virgin?"

He nodded. "And a feeling that I had always been your lover, and that each time I made love to you for the first time, you were always a virgin."

I was waiting for him. The thought flashed in and out of her mind. But how else could she explain her still being a virgin at her age?

"That's nonsense, Caleb." Her voice shook. "To do what you do, you must have a grounding in the sciences. In fact I think I read in that article that you do."

"Yes, but I also have a great fascination and respect for the unknown. It would be tough to do what I do if I let myself get bogged down in absolutes."

She came up on her elbow, causing her hair to cascade down over her left shoulder and over one

breast. "Yeah, but it seems to me that things, whatever they are, would have to make sense to you."

"Most of the time that's true, but some things
are just never going to make sense, Joy, no matter
how hard you try. And if you keep insisting that they
must, you're going to miss out on a lot in life." He
watched her, aching to reach out and take her in his
arms. But he resisted because he understood. She
was trying to work through what was happening
between them, and he had to respect that. "Has
your whole life made sense?"

"Most of it," she murmured. But not all of it.
Within two months of her father's death her mother
died in a car crash in France. "And what hasn't made
sense has ended badly."

"You and I won't end badly."

"I know that." She knew that because she didn't
plan to leave the matter to chance. She was going to
say good-bye to him. Soon. In fact she would do it
the minute Grace came back. When that happened,
she could return to her own life. But in the meantime she had a few more days. . . . "How do you
know we won't end badly?"

"Because I have this very certain feeling."

He was wrong, she thought with a tinge of des-
peration. He had to be, or else the way she had led
her life up to now was completely wrong. But, no, it
couldn't be. She had saved a great many men from

hurt, and had had a lot of fun in the process. And what could be wrong about that?

Nothing made sense anymore. She had no doubt that in the future it would, but for now it didn't.

She reached out to him, running her hand across his chest, touching his nipples, lingering, exploring. He caught her hand and looked at her questioningly.

"Be with me in this life right now," she whispered, "at least for just a little longer."

"I'll always be with you," he said, pulling her to him.

When the dawn broke, lightening the gold color of the bed's draperies around them, they were still locked together in an embrace.

NINE

"I'm at an antique store, Molly, and I will be all day, so cancel everything you've got for me." As Caleb listened to Molly's reply to him, he pulled out a drawer from Grace's desk, leaned back in the chair, and propped his feet atop the drawer. "Yep, I said all day." He sent a warm, lazy grin over at Joy, who was brewing the tea for the morning.

"Aw, come on, Molly, they're fascinating places, even if they do only play classical music. I tell you what I'll do. I'll give you next Wednesday off—mark it down and don't forget to remind me—and then you can spend the day in an antique shop of your choice and see exactly what I mean."

His grin widened as he jerked the phone away from his ear and held it out. Molly's opinion of his idea came out of the receiver loud and clear. Joy couldn't help but return Caleb's grin.

Caleb let his administrative assistant rant on a little while longer, then brought the phone back to his ear, his grin as wide as ever. "Okay, Molly. Okay. You don't have to take a day off if you don't want to, and even if you did want to, I of course understand that you certainly don't have to spend it in an antique shop. It was a bad suggestion." He listened for a minute, then threw back his head and laughed out loud. "Well, I wouldn't say it was *that* bad, Molly."

Joy watched him as she went about Grace's morning routine of turning on the lights and the music, making the coffee and the tea, refreshing the potpourri, plus all the other little touches that Grace made a point of doing. Luckily the routine required no concentration. Luckily, because she couldn't tear her gaze or her mind from Caleb.

An elegant line drawing of a man playing a guitar graced the front of his T-shirt. On the back, inside a small square, the words ERIC CLAPTON WORLD TOUR were printed. Black jeans clung softly to Caleb's long legs. The black sport coat he had carried in and flung over a chair had landed so that she could read the label. *Armani.*

Somehow, some way, *still* he engendered a mix of protectiveness and need inside her, and she was having to fight against the desire to go over and curl up in his lap.

How did he do it? How did he make her want him, even when he was talking to someone else on the phone?

He didn't operate like anyone she had ever known. If he had rules, she had yet to discover any. When she told him to leave, he ignored her, just as he did when she told him she wanted to leave. And when he made love to her, he could make the whole world go away, until there were only the two of them and red-hot fire. . . .

He threw a quick glance at her, as if to reassure himself she was still there, then brought his gaze back to the absent contemplation of his scuffed tennis shoes. "So what else do you want to yell at me about? You've got"—he checked his watch—"thirty seconds. Go."

He listened for a few seconds, then began to answer her. "Cancel. Cancel. Just put both of those on the back burner for now. Move that one to next week. Uh-huh. Right. Call him back and tell him, 'Sorry, can't do it.' Ignore him. Ignore her too. Yeah, okay, call him back and tell him I'll get in touch with him by the end of the week, then remind me. No, can't do that. Yeah, yeah, uh-huh. Okay, just R.S.V.P. my regrets on everything else. Have you heard from Larry? Good. Put him at the top of my list to get back to. That it? Anything else? Good. Okay . . . oh, by the way, Daisy's at her house in

Austin, just so you know. Listen, I'm pulling up the drawbridge for an unspecified length of time. You know the emergency numbers if you need me. Otherwise I'll check back with you in a few days. Hey, and thanks a bunch." He hung up the phone and immediately looked around for her.

"Molly must be quite a lady to put up with you. It can't be easy to work for a man who's never there."

"My company is designed to give me maximum freedom, and if she needed to, Molly could run the world without any help at all."

She strolled slowly toward him. "It must be nice to be able to pull up the drawbridge whenever you want."

"You've never done that? Draw the drapes? Unplug the phone? Pretend you're not home? Either that, or take off without telling anyone where you're going or when you'll be back?"

"No, but then I guess I've never wanted to badly enough. Not really."

"Everyone needs an escape system. For instance, by doing this for your sister you're giving her one."

"She's not escaping. She's working."

"Usually so am I."

Stopping herself just short of sitting down on his lap, she perched on the corner of the desk. "And what are you doing now? Why did you pull up the drawbridge this time?"

He smiled. "Don't you know? I want to spend some time with you, and I want to help you."

Silver-blue light glistened in his eyes, beckoning. She shouldn't have to fight her feelings for him so much, she thought. She shouldn't *have* any feelings.

Searching for something constructive to do, she reached for his glasses and cleaned their lenses with the lace edge of her slip. "Help me what?"

He grasped her hand and drew her off her perch and down onto his lap. "Help you with anything you'd like."

She slipped his glasses back on him. "I don't need any help."

"Last night you were concerned about something going on with Grace's business. Have you changed your mind?"

"Far from it. I've been trying to decide where to start, that's all."

"And have you decided?"

"Sort of. The antiques business, more than others, is built on reputation. I can't risk going to anyone to authenticate the returned pieces, because I don't want even a hint to get out that something's wrong. Besides, I have no idea who Grace would go to for something like that. But I could start with checking the documentation on the returned pieces, plus the sewing table that both Bertrand and Daisy have commented on. Maybe I'll find some sort of link."

"And if you don't, then what?"

"I have no idea."

"Are you sure you don't want to take a wait-and-see attitude?"

She shook her head. "I can't. It's just not in me to sit here and do nothing. I may not be able to accomplish a thing, but I'll feel a whole lot better going on the offensive." Maybe it was even more than that, she thought. Maybe she needed a puzzle to keep her mind off what was an ever greater puzzle: Caleb and her. Unfortunately an answer to Grace's puzzle wouldn't give her an answer to the puzzle of her and Caleb. "With just a little digging I may be able to come up with a very simple answer. That way everything will be fine by the time Grace comes home."

"And if the answer isn't simple?"

"Then all the more reason for me to find out, don't you think? Maybe there's something I can do to stop it before the problem becomes too volatile for anyone to handle."

He chuckled tenderly. "If I'm ever in any trouble, I want you on my side."

She gave in to the urge that had predominated

since he'd pulled her down onto his lap and slipped her arm around his neck. "I wouldn't be so quick to say that," she said, combing her fingers through his hair with a need to touch and straighten. "I wasn't able to save you from the wagon train." She couldn't begin to explain why she had said such a stupid thing, and for the moment she didn't try.

"Ah, but you saved me from the Buick, so it's all right." He bent his head and gave her a brief but hot kiss. "Okay, then let's do this. Where's Grace's computer?"

She pressed a hand to her still-tingling lips, wondering why she couldn't seem to recover as quickly as he did from their kisses. "She keeps it in the back," she said, her voice husky. "I'll get it. It's a lightweight laptop."

Instead of releasing her from his hold, he skimmed his hand up and down her leg in a manner that evoked memories of the night that had just passed, when his hands had been all over her and she had loved every minute of it.

She was losing, Joy thought, and she didn't even remember agreeing to play the game.

"Grace doesn't keep the computer out here," she said, in an effort to get back to the problem at hand, "because it interferes with the old-fashioned, another-time ambience she has here in the shop."

She slipped from his lap, but he caught her hand. "Let me help you."

"No, that's okay. Besides, I also need to get her disks. They're in her safe, and while I trust you, I don't think it would be right to show you her combination without her permission."

His hand tightened on hers. "You trust me?"

She looked down at him. "Trust you?" Lord, help her, she had definitely said those words. "Yes," she said slowly. "Yes, I suppose I do."

He surged to his feet. "You didn't say *suppose*. You said you did. Do you?"

"Yes." She had no idea when or how her trust of him had come about, but, she realized, she *did* trust him.

"Thank you." He bent his head and pressed a long kiss to her mouth.

She pushed a hand against his shoulder to create a little more space between them. She felt in dire need of breathing room. "Don't read too much into my trusting you, Caleb. You're an easy man to trust."

He laughed, delighted. "Is that so? And does that mean you don't really think I'm weird?"

"No, I think you're weird."

He took her hand in his. "Your trust means more than you'll ever know, Joy."

She shrugged, trying to make light of it. "I

would never have gone to bed with you if I hadn't trusted you."

His eyes took on their familiar twinkle. "And did I live up to your expectations in that regard?"

Pulling her hands away, she rolled her eyes. "Oh, pu-*leeze*. You want *compliments*? I wouldn't be surprised to know that the bed levitated last night."

"It did."

He would have to go a long way to look any more satisfied with himself, she thought, disgruntled. But then, she had to admit that it had certainly felt to her as if the bed had levitated. Then again, maybe it had just been *she* who had levitated. "I'll be right back."

A few minutes later she was staring warily at Grace's laptop computer as Caleb connected a cord to its back, then plugged in the other end to a socket. "Lord, but I hate computers."

He laughed. "A computer is your friend, Joy."

"Says who?"

"Says the people who make them."

"Exactly."

"But it is the truth." He settled himself in front of the computer and turned it on. "Frankly I don't know how you run your business without one."

"I hire an accountant to keep my books. I give him copies of all my receipts, and he gives me a printout once a week of my inventory and my bank balance. And in between times I use a pencil and an eraser. It worked for my grandfather, and it works for me."

"I bet I could have you using one in only a few—"

Her chuckle interrupted him. "No, you couldn't, no matter *what* amount of time you have in mind, because I don't *want* to know how."

He laughed again. "Yeah, that's what you said about the abacus too."

"*Don't*," she said warningly. "I don't want to hear it." She was doing everything in her power *not* to think about his notion that they had loved each other in other lives.

She scooped up a stack of three-and-a-half-inch disks from the corner of the desk where she'd placed them and handed them to him. Then she put a sheet of paper on which she had written all the information she had on the three antiques beside him.

He shuffled through the disks, reading the labels, then inserted one and began punching keys. "It doesn't make sense to me that the two items that have been returned were fakes," she said. "Grace simply wouldn't mistake a fake or a reproduction for an antique."

"You may be exactly right. For instance, have you considered that the first lady who came in could be friends with the couple that came in yesterday? Their confidence could have been shaken by hers."

Joy's mouth tightened. "Nothing—and any-thing—makes sense at this point. It's even possible that Bertrand is somehow behind all this in an attempt to discredit Grace."

"Do you really think that?"

"I wouldn't put it past him, but on the other hand I have no idea how he could be doing it."

"Well, we'll just have to see if we can figure it out."

We. He had said *we*. She swallowed against a dry throat. She was trying so hard to avoid hurt, but she hurt at just the thought of no longer being with him.

He punched a final series of keys, then sat back. "Okay, I'm into her system, and I've found the three pieces."

"Wait a minute. I forgot to give you her password."

"Like I said, I'm in her system."

"Just like that?"

"Just like that."

She blew out a long breath and peered over his shoulder. "Okay, we need to find out if the three pieces have anything in common. Start with the basics. Origin and period of each piece."

After a minute he shook his head. "All three came from different places, and they were of different periods."

She straightened away from him, unable to continue inhaling with any equanimity the clean, faintly musky scent that emanated from him. It was a scent that seemed to surround her constantly, when she dreamed, when she made love to him. . . .

She frowned. "I was really counting on finding out they had all come from the same place. It would make sense, but . . . okay, let's try cost, then shippers."

A short time later Caleb was again shaking his head. "Grace paid a goodly price for them. They were no bargains, and as for the shippers"—he hit a key, then another—"two of the three were sent here by the same shipper."

"Which two?"

"The Regency sofa table and the sewing table."

"What about the dates that she purchased them? And then check the dates she sold them." She waited while his fingers ran over the keyboard, causing the keys to click rapidly.

"Well," he said after a moment, "she bought all three pieces within two month's time of each other, had them in inventory for several months, and then sold them within a couple of days of each other." He made an approving sound. "Your sister has a nice profit margin."

"Nothing more than what is fair."

"I wasn't criticizing." He sent her an understanding smile, then looked back at the screen.

"Wait a minute." He punched several more keys. "They were all refinished by the same company. Does Grace automatically have every piece she purchases refinished?"

She shook her head. "No. Some don't need it. Others she knows will appeal more to the customers if she leaves them the way she found them." She thought for a moment. "You met the owner of the company at the auction—remember? Robert London. I wonder if Bertrand recommended London's to Grace. Right before we went upstairs, Robert said he was going to talk to Bertrand."

Caleb still studied the screen. "All three pieces were bought within the last seven months and sent to the refinisher's. The Regency table and the secretaire sold within a few days of her receiving them back from the refinisher's, but as we know, she still has the sewing table."

"That's interesting. Maybe I should pay Robert London a visit."

He leaned back in the chair and eyed her with weary resignation. "I don't like the sound of that."

"Look, I figured out a possible connection, but nothing more than that. It's really just a suspicion, nothing concrete. If only I knew more about antiques. Waylon delivered a tea table yesterday from London's. I wonder—"

"You can examine the tea table if you want, but it

didn't look that expensive to me, and I've found one more thing all three pieces have in common—they are all extremely expensive."

Her eyes widened with excitement. "That makes sense. *If* London's is duplicating Grace's antiques, returning the fakes to her, then selling the real pieces off for what I assume has to be a huge profit, it makes sense that they would only duplicate the costly items."

She waved a hand toward the computer. "Can you find me a piece or two that Grace has placed with them but hasn't received back yet? Something expensive."

"I can make this baby sing 'Ave Maria' if you want."

"I'll save that little treat for Christmas. For now all I want is the information."

"I'll remember that at Christmastime." A chuckle spiced his mock-threatening tone. After several moments' work he said, "Okay, I've got one here."

"Good, let me copy down the details and then let's go."

"Are you going to do your Grace act?"

"That's right," she said evenly, reaching for a pad and pencil, "and if you come along, you're going to do your chauffeur act."

"But I don't have a chauffeur act."

"Do you want to come with me or not?"

He exhaled a long breath. "I guess that means I've got to find my keys."

"On the table near the front door."

"Really? How did they get there?"

"Guess," she said, copying down the information she would need.

Caleb watched as Joy shook hands with Robert London, presumably saying good-bye. From his viewpoint it appeared London was gazing at Joy with all the hunger of a man who'd been deprived of sweets his whole life. London would get a bite of Joy over his dead body, he thought grimly.

It had been hard as hell to sit here, doing nothing, while she had gone in alone. The lines and figures on the legal yellow pad in his lap attested to his attempt to keep his sanity. Not that he had thought for a minute that she was in danger. From his observations of the last fifteen minutes London's was run like any other business, with people going in and out on a more or less regular basis. But seeing her on his way back to him, he couldn't help but feel better. His gaze returned to the building behind her. There was something about it. . . .

"I didn't see anything out of line," she said with disgust, climbing into the car.

He reached out and stroked his hand down her hair, simply enjoying the contact. "What did you expect? A sign saying, WE COPY FURNITURE HERE?"

"It would have been helpful." She waved a hand behind her, indicating the direction from which she had just come. "He took me on a complete tour, including the back, where they do the refinishing. The fumes nearly knocked me off my feet."

"Were there areas he kept off limits to you?"

She shook her head. "No. I saw every step of the process." She pointed to a row of ground-level windows along the front of the building. "That's Robert's office. A very nice reception area adjoins it. The rest is where they actually do the refinishing."

He nodded. "Did you see the piece that belongs to your sister?"

"Sure did. It's nearly ready. As I said, everything looked on the up and up and very prosperous. There is even new equipment sitting about still in the crates. All the areas were extremely neat." She rubbed her arms. "But you know, I got a funny feeling. . . . I have no idea what it could be though. Robert couldn't have been more charming." Caleb made a sound of disgust, drawing her attention, and she saw that he had been doing some figuring on one of his ever-present legal pads. "What are you doing?"

"I have a funny feeling too." Almost compulsively he pressed a quick kiss on her lips, then handed her the legal pad. "Maybe it's nothing, but while it's fresh in your mind, draw what you remember of the building. I know the proportions will probably be off, but do the best you can. Think about what you actually saw and how large each area looked to you."

A short time later she returned his pad to him. "There it is."

He looked at her drawing, then back at the building. It was a large one-story, high-ceiling, sprawling brick warehouse with the windows along one side painted cream so that people couldn't look in. A large ventilation fan turned slowly near the roof. "According to your drawing, there's an area you didn't see. In fact I'd say the space comprises about one third of the building, and it appears to me that it runs down that side there." He pointed.

She gazed thoughtfully at the building. "I think you're right. The back room I was shown where the refinishing is being done looks from the inside as if it extends all the way across the building, but now I don't think it does. There must be some way to find out for sure."

Caleb shook his head and started the car. "Short of breaking and entering, I don't think so."

"Maybe I wouldn't have to," she said, craning her neck to check out the cream-colored windows that marched down the side of the building about eight feet off the ground. "Maybe I could just look."

Some hours later the sky was darkening behind him as Caleb quietly chuckled. He and Joy were squatted down behind a big green Dumpster. The large trash receptacle belonged to the building that sat across the parking lot from the London Refinishing Company. "Do you realize how ludicrous this is?" he asked her.

Her lips twisted ruefully. "Believe me, I do, but I just feel so much better doing something, *anything*, even if it's this." She waved her hand, indicating the Dumpster. "You didn't have to come, you know."

"Did you really think I'd let you come alone?"

She glanced at him. "No." Somehow she had known he would come with her, even in the face of her protestations. And somehow she had known she would be glad to have him with her. And she was. She definitely was. She checked her watch. It was almost eight o'clock. "I counted a dozen employees when I was in there. I've counted eleven who have left. We'll wait a little bit longer, and then—" She gave a soft exclamation. "There goes the twelfth."

"You know that they're bound to have security in there, don't you?"

"Yeah, I know, but all we need is just a quick look."

He smiled. He was fully aware that she was using her sister's problem as a shield against having to think about the two of them. Whatever was happening in her sister's business was not a matter of life-and-death and could easily wait until Grace got home. And the problem most assuredly didn't call for them to squat behind a Dumpster like two criminals, trying to figure a way to get a look inside the building.

He'd give her this little caper, he thought, mainly because he believed that forcing the issue and telling her too soon that he loved her would be a mistake. But as soon as Grace was home and Joy's life was back to whatever she called normal, he planned to find a convenient corner and back her into it regarding their relationship.

"Give me a few minutes," he said, "and I can dismantle their security system."

"No," she said, truly horrified at the thought of him putting himself in any kind of jeopardy. "That's against the law, plus too risky."

"Okay, then I have another idea."

"What?"

He slipped his hand into the pocket of his Armani jacket and brought out a baseball. "When we were driving away this afternoon, I noticed some kids playing baseball a few blocks down. And when kids play baseball, it's not out of the ordinary for windows to get broken. And when it's done on purpose, it's only criminal mischief. But if we don't get caught, it's not even that."

Her mouth dropped open in delight. "Caleb, you're a *genius*."

"That's what they say."

She leaned over and kissed him, unconscious of the fact that it was the first time she had ever initiated a kiss. Caleb, however, was very aware of it.

She rushed on. "A baseball will also draw out anyone who's inside the building. That way we can tell how many guys we're up against. Give me the baseball."

"Hold it!" He put a detaining hand on her arm. "*I'm* going to throw the baseball and hopefully make a decent-sized hole that *I* can look into *very* briefly. After that we're out of here. Right?"

"That's fine, Caleb, except the last time I looked, you weren't eight feet tall, which is how high those windows are."

After making a quick visual check of the window's height, something he hadn't thought to do before, he grimaced. "All right," he said grudgingly. "I'll lift you, but you've got sixty seconds, and that's it."

She made a noncommittal gesture. "By the way, where did you get the baseball?"

"While you were waiting on Mr. and Mrs. Stevenson this afternoon, I went out and bought it, along with this." He reached into the pocket of his jacket and drew out a flashlight. "It's small, but it's powerful."

Her mouth dropped open in amazement. "You *do* pay attention to details."

With a chuckle he stood. "When they matter. Stay here." Caleb crossed halfway across the parking lot, took aim, and threw. The ball sailed through a lower pane of a window with a satisfying crash. He ran back to the Dumpster and sank down beside Joy.

Within a very short time two men came running out to the side parking lot, one of them carrying a baseball.

"Damn kids," the older one said. "I've seen them around the neighborhood. They got too close this time." His eyes scanned the lot. "I guess they're long gone by now."

"I sure would be," the younger one said with a half grin. "Look, it's too late to buy a replacement glass tonight, but I'll get on it first thing in the morning. Fortunately it's supposed to be a clear night, so we don't have to worry about rain."

The older of the two men tossed the ball up and

caught it, his expression still disgusted. "Yeah, I guess. Come on, let's go back in."

Caleb took Joy's hand and pulled her out from behind the Dumpster. "Let's get this over with."

Beneath the window he took her by the waist, and as they had the first day they met, he lifted her.

Joy balanced herself, then reached out for the ledge of the window and peered through the hole that had been made by the baseball.

There were several low-wattage security lights on in the large space, but with the flashlight she could make out objects fairly well. There were several kinds of woodworking equipment, along with crates, which she assumed contained more machinery. Workbenches lined one wall and held a large variety of tools. Wood was racked according to size and type, and cans of paint, varnish, and stain were stacked neatly in shelves.

And in the center of the room stood a large antique chest. Not too far away sat another, except that it lacked hardware and stain. Although she couldn't be entirely certain, it appeared to her that the duplicate would look exactly like the original once the stain had been applied and the hardware put on.

But then she saw something that she recognized without a doubt: the Regency mahogany sideboard that Grace loved so much and used for the coffee and tea. She remembered now: Grace had told her that it was a one-of-a-kind piece, and once it had come back from the refinisher's, Grace had put a small NOT FOR SALE sign on it. *It had to be a fake*. The one she was looking at must be the *real* antique.

"I've seen enough," Joy whispered. "Let's go."

"They're definitely building furniture in there," she said as they drove away, "and it looks as if they're building it to pass off as the real thing. We won't be able to tell, of course, until someone gets in there and does a search to get absolute proof—"

"Not us," Caleb said quickly, interrupting.

"No, I agree. It's time to go to the police, tell them what we know, and get them to search."

He shook his head. "I agree, but it won't be easy. It'll be our word against Robert London's."

"I think our combined reputations should help us along. I mean, we're both local business owners."

"Yeah, except you're pretending to be your sister, and we just broke at least one law back there, namely criminal mischief, maybe two if you count trespassing."

"Oh, well," she said, shrugging. "What's a few broken laws when we're talking about a huge scam. Plus, if the police will just go in and seize the real sideboard, I think we'll have them."

"I hope you're right."

TEN

Joy looked carefully around her, then set the extension ladder she had brought with her beneath the warehouse window Caleb had broken earlier in the day. She had left him at his house, involved in a telephone call. He believed she was using this time to go back to Grace's, check on messages, and pick up a fresh set of clothes. And she *had* gone to Grace's, but she had picked up the ladder and a camera.

She had had no choice. The police had in effect stonewalled them. Oh, they had been very polite, listening to what both she and Caleb had had to say, but in the end she had received the distinct impression that the police were going to do nothing, and she didn't understand it.

She had tried her best to let the matter go, telling herself that the situation would wait until Grace got home. But all evening she had found herself feeling anxious, even through a lovely dinner with Caleb. And the anxious feeling had grown until she had known that she had to go back to the warehouse.

She climbed the ladder, careful to keep a good grip on the camera. When she reached the top, she took one more look around the parking lot. Blessedly it was quiet.

She positioned the camera and started taking pictures. Surely, she thought, this would give the police enough evidence so that they would issue a search warrant.

The flash went off time after time as she pressed the shutter. She had taken about a dozen shots when she felt the ladder shake. And then she was falling, right into a pair of strong arms.

Except they weren't Caleb's arms.

She looked up into the grim face of one of the security guards she had seen earlier. And then from a few feet away she heard the voice of Robert London. "Why don't you come in and visit with us awhile, Grace?"

She had no choice. Since the security guard didn't put her down until they reached Robert London's office, she had no choice but to comply.

"Well, Grace," London said as soon as she was set on her feet, "to what do we owe the pleasure?"

"Oh, knock it off, Robert." Her tone was probably sharper than was strictly prudent, given the circumstances, she reflected ruefully. But she was angry at herself for getting caught. He was looking at her with some surprise, and she realized that at least to his mind she probably wasn't acting very much like her sister. Luckily he didn't know her or Grace that well. "I suppose it wouldn't do any good to say that if you let me go, I won't mention any of this."

London sank into the chair behind his desk, Grace's camera in his hand. "Say anything you like. You have a lovely voice, and I enjoy hearing you talk."

He didn't seem very upset that she was here. Why? It didn't make any sense. "Someone *does* know exactly where I am."

He bestowed a charming smile on her, one that would have seemed appropriate at an auction or a party. "Of course they do. Won't you sit down?"

"You don't believe me?"

"I would never call a beautiful lady a liar. I would also never hold a beautiful lady's property longer than necessary." He flicked open the camera, tugged out the film cartridge, and held out the empty camera to her. When she didn't take it, he set it down.

"Dammit it, Robert," she said loudly, "what's going on here?"

"Try not to raise your voice, Grace. Troy, there, is kind of nervous."

She threw a glance over her shoulder to the grim-faced security guard. "Excuse me, Troy, but I've never been in this particular position before."

"He understands."

Just in time she stopped a disparaging remark about Troy's intelligence from leaving her mouth. "Where is the other security guard?"

"He's around." London smiled. "As to what is going on, Grace? Exactly what you've already figured out. But it's really nothing for you to worry about."

"I think you should be the one who is worried," she said, throwing an absent glance at the surface of the desk. There was a water bottle, a set of bookends supporting several hardcover books, a few papers. Why, she wondered, was she looking at the desk?

"No, I don't think so. We were about to fold up our tent and steal away into the night anyway. We've had a good run here, but it's time to move on and set up someplace else. Your visit has simply hastened our departure."

"The crates," she said, more to herself than to him. Earlier that day she had seen the crates and assumed the company had bought new pieces of equipment. Instead they must have packed up most of their existing equipment in preparation for their move, and subconsciously she must have sensed that. It explained the reason for the anxiousness she had felt to get back here.

He waved a hand toward a chair. "Make yourself comfortable. As I said, you're going to be here awhile, just until we can get out of here. Once we're gone, there'll be no evidence, and you can say whatever you like to whomever you like."

Good, she thought. She had time, time to try to formulate some kind of plan, time to try *not* to think of Caleb and wish with everything that was in her she hadn't left him, time to wish she didn't love him. . . .

She was shaking when she turned her gaze back on Robert. "You're wrong about there being no evidence. I saw the original Regency sideboard through the window. The fake sideboard is back at the shop, and that, Robert, is evidence."

"You have a fake sideboard? I'm really sorry to hear that. I bet it must have cost a lot of money too. People aren't going to think well of you, Grace, when they hear that you bought a fake sideboard."

"You know well enough that the sideboard I bought was authentic."

"Do I? Prove it."

"Now that I know what's going on, I will."

"Really? How?"

"I have the fake. Even if you manage to leave, I'll

track you and the original down. If you sell it, I'll put the word out in antique circles."

Robert shook his head with mock regret. "It won't do you any good. Since I know you've seen the original, I'm going to have Tony destroy the original. We've got a sledgehammer that will have it reduced to toothpicks in ten minutes."

She gasped in horror. "You'd destroy it!"

"Not willingly, but it seems I have no other choice."

Cold panic slid down her spin. There wasn't going to be any time, she thought frantically. They would destroy the sideboard and be gone before she could get help, and then there would be no way she could save Grace's reputation.

Heavy green velvet drapes. She glanced toward the blue-curtained window. Idly she reached for the bookend, not even sure why she was doing it. It was a brass eagle, probably very expensive.

An inkwell, a lamp, its flame flickering, a derringer, Caleb . . .

"Put that back, Grace, and sit down."

"What?"

She had loved him then. She loved him now.

"Grace, put it back and sit down, dammit. We need to talk. . . ."

Dazed by the images and thoughts, she looked at Robert and saw him talking to her. Why had she picked up the eagle?

She looked back at the curtains. Without thinking, she suddenly whirled and threw the eagle as hard as she could at Troy, who was still standing in the doorway. Just at that moment there was a loud crash, and something came through the window wrapped in the curtain.

With a curse London turned toward the window, but it was too late. Caleb appeared from behind the curtain and knocked him down with an upper cut to the jaw. He threw a quick glance over his shoulder and saw that Joy was struggling in the guard's arms.

"Dammit, let her go!"

In the midst of the struggle and anxiety a pistol cocked, and a tall man in a rumpled sport coat, carrying the pistol, stepped into the room. *"Police. You're all under arrest."*

Joy landed an elbow against the security guard's stomach, freeing herself. As he folded forward, she launched herself into Caleb's arms.

He caught her and tightly hugged her to him. Over her head he saw another policeman enter the room. "We're under arrest too?"

"For the present, until we sort out who's who."

The big four-poster bed with its golden canopy and concealing drapes had never seemed more comfortable or havenlike. A couple of hours had passed since Caleb had crashed through the warehouse window, and the confusion and fright of that moment had faded.

Content and happy, Joy snuggled back against the pillows. "I can't believe the police were onto London's the whole time. I mean, they could have told us."

Beside her, Caleb took her hand and laced his fingers with hers. There had been a time of sheer terror for him tonight, a time when he wasn't sure what was happening to Joy inside the warehouse. Now that she was here with him, safe, it might not be possible for him to ever let her out of his sight again.

"The police were hoping, once we saw we weren't going to get any cooperation from them, that we'd have enough sense to leave the situation alone. They had the place staked out, and when they saw me throw the ball through the window, they didn't know what the hell we were doing." He chuckled. "They just wanted us to go away and leave them to their business."

"Thank goodness they were watching," she said feelingly. "Thank goodness they saw Troy carrying me in and decided they'd better move in."

Thank goodness. The two words seemed to explode from the depths of his heart.

A tear slipped from her eye, and she quickly wiped it away. She'd been in no real danger tonight, yet she'd felt an excruciating danger in being parted from Caleb. It had had something to do with what was happening inside her, rather than what was happening around her.

And just as she had sensed a moment before it happened, Caleb had reached her first, before the policeman.

With her fingers locked with his, she curled his hand toward her until it rested against her heart. There was so much she needed to say to him, but working through it all and finding the right words, along with the courage, was coming hard.

"The really amazing thing to me is that Bertrand was helping the police," she said quietly. "He had secretly marked and carefully documented several pieces of furniture and sent them to London's to try to provide the police with the irrefutable evidence they needed. He chose the pieces that he deemed would be the ones most likely to be copied, and he chose more than one so that Robert couldn't claim the copy was accidental. It must have been why he suggested I put the tea table in the back. In his own way he was trying to protect me." She shook her head. "I mean, Grace."

"Have you called her yet?"

She nodded. "While you were talking to Daisy. I

told Grace everything. She'll be back day after to-morrow."

"Do you think the coup she has managed to pull off will end the rivalry between her and Bertrand?"

"I don't know. It's hard to say. She's very grate-ful to him for his help in trying to uncover the scam, and at the same time I know he'll have a greater respect for her professionally. But—"

"Old habits die hard?"

A small smile curved her lips. "Exactly."

"Like you and me."

The smile faded. *Habits of other lifetimes.* How could any rational person accept that concept?

She frowned down at their joined hands. "I'm confused about something, Caleb. I know why the police showed up, but what about you? I left you here on the telephone."

His lips twisted wryly. "You're not going to like the explanation."

"Tell me anyway."

"A few minutes after you left to go to Grace's, it occurred to me that in the past when we've been in similar circumstances, you've always gone to the exact place I didn't want you to go."

"You're talking about similar circumstances in the really *distant* past, aren't you? As in other lives."

He nodded, watching her closely. "See. I told you you wouldn't like my explanation."

"It's not that I don't like it, it's that I don't understand it."

"Then let's go at this another way. Why did you throw the bookend?"

"That's easy. It was self-defense."

The doubting look on his face urged her to rethink her answer

"I really don't know, Caleb." After a moment's further thought, she went on, "I had these flashes of objects, and somehow I knew you'd come in that window."

"I was compelled to go through that window. I knew you were on the other side."

There was no understanding any of it, she thought, no matter how hard she tried. And in the end, when all was said and done, there was only one thing that was really clear. She didn't want to live her life without Caleb.

She came up on her knees, twisting around so that she faced him. "I've fought this long enough. I'm making a decision right here and now. I'm going to stop putting barriers between you and me. One of these days I'll tell you about my parents, but for now I'm not going to worry any longer about what happened between them all those years ago. That was their life. This is mine. And maybe you and I *were* together in other lifetimes. Maybe we weren't. But I don't think it matters. It only matters what happens in *this* lifetime." She framed his face with her hands. "And in this lifetime, Caleb McClintock, I love you. I love you very much."

He gently drew her down against him and kissed her with a tenderness and a passion that had them both shaking. "I love you, too, and have right from the beginning. But you know that, don't you?"

"Yes, I do."

"If we don't get it right this lifetime," he whispered against her mouth, "we will the next. We've got all of eternity."

She smiled tremulously, wrapped her arms around his neck, and rolled until she was lying on her back and he was half over her. Threading her fingers up through his hair, she whispered, "Something tells me we're going to get it right this time."

THE EDITOR'S CORNER

Dear Readers,

If you loved our **BAD BOYS** last year, wait till you get a taste of our November LOVESWEPTs: **DANGEROUS MEN!** From a mysterious under-cover state trooper to a roguish football player and a wilder-than-wild oil field wildcatter, these men thrive on danger, live on the edge, and push passion right past the limit! Like our heroines, you'll find it impos-sible to resist the sheer thrill of a walk on the wild side with men who are definitely *not* what your mother had in mind! With bold seduction and promises of passion, November's six heroes will sweep our hero-ines—and you—off your feet and into the fantasy of being loved by a Dangerous Man. . . .

Leanne Banks has created our first Dangerous Man in the sultry tale she calls **DANCE WITH THE DEVIL**, LOVESWEPT #648. Garth Pendleton was a bad boy who was definitely out of Erin Lindsey's league. Everything about him was a dare and Erin trembled at the danger of caring for a man whose darkest secret was tangled with her own shadowed past. Garth felt he'd waited for Erin forever and wanted to give her back her lost dreams, but if she knew the pain that haunted him, he feared the woman who'd slipped inside his lonely heart might slip away. This tempting tale is sure to please all of you who helped to make Leanne's January 1993 LOVESWEPT a #1 bestseller.

Doris Parmett's electrifying heroes and heroines have never been so highly-charged as they are in **BAD ATTITUDE**, LOVESWEPT #649. Reid Cameron was a heartbreaker cop who kissed like the hero of a hot romance. He'd invaded Polly Sweet's privacy—and her fantasies—when he'd commandeered her house to catch a jewel thief, but when he decided they'd play lovers and then tried to teach the feisty spitfire a lesson about feigning passion, both were shocked by the fireworks their lips set off! Doris is in top form with this sizzling story.

Longtime favorite author Patt Bucheister will tempt and tease you to distraction with her **TAME A WILDCAT**, LOVESWEPT #650. Ryder Knight had always thrived on the adventure of being a wildcatter, relished the pursuit of a new oil well, but he felt his restlessness vanish when Hannah Corbett told him he looked like trouble—and that he was no gentleman! But when his possessive embrace made her go up in flames, she feared losing control, trading her freedom for the joy only he could teach her. Patt will keep you on the edge of your seat for every page of this one!

We at LOVESWEPT are always pleased to welcome a talented new writer to our pages, and we're sure you'll agree that Donna Kauffman, author of

ILLEGAL MOTION, LOVESWEPT #651, is as good as they come. Football star Nick Logan was desperate enough to try anything to clear his name, and he figured he could intimidate or charm the truth out of Willa Trask—until he was burned by the sparks that flared between him and the beautiful redhead! He'd hired her to rehabilitate his injured knee, vowing to discover if she'd helped frame him—but instead of an ice princess, he found in her a wanton witch who touched his soul. When you've read this winning story, I'm sure you'll become big fans of Donna Kauffman!

We turn from a rookie to an all-star pro for our next Dangerous Man. Let the heartbreaking emotion of Laura Taylor sweep you away with **WILDER'S WOMAN**, LOVESWEPT #652. Craig Wilder— uncivilized, untamed, he'd paid a high price for survival. He'd meant to teach Chelsea Lockridge a lesson, to punish his ex-wife for her betrayal, but he hadn't anticipated the erotic torment of molding his body to hers—nor imagined the tenderness still buried deep inside his battered heart! She'd braved the wilderness and a storm with evidence that could deliver the justice Craig had been denied, but Chelsea wanted to prove she'd never lost faith in him . . . or her reckless passion for the man who could make her purr with pleasure. Branded for all eternity by a lover whose scars ran deep, she vowed she could help Craig mourn the past and trust her again by fighting his demons with the sweet fury of her love. Laura's deeply moving tale will capture you, heart and soul.

If you like your men *truly* dangerous, Glenna McReynolds has the mystery man for you in **AVENGING ANGEL**, LOVESWEPT #653. Bruised and bloody, Dylan Jones has driven a thousand miles with her name on his lips, desperate to save Johanna Lane from being murdered! The secrets she knew made her a target, and he was her best chance of getting out alive—even if it meant abducting the lady and keeping her with him against her will. Frightened and furious, Johanna was stunned to realize she knew her captor . . . and once had even desired him! Dylan gambled his life to feel her heat and taste the forbidden fruit of her lips and Johanna longed to repay the debt. I can't think of a better way to end your month of **DANGEROUS MEN** than with Glenna's **AVENGING ANGEL**!

So hang on to your hearts—next month six **DANGEROUS MEN** are coming to steal them away!

Happy reading,

Nita Taublib

Nita Taublib

Associate Publisher

P.S. Don't miss the exciting women's fiction Bantam has coming in November—sensual seduction in Susan Johnson's **OUTLAW**; love and black magic over the centuries in **MOONLIGHT, MADNESS, AND MAGIC** by LOVESWEPT authors Suzanne Forster, Charlotte Hughes, and Olivia Rupprecht; and a classic Fayrene Preston romance, **SATIN AND STEELE**. We'll be giving you a sneak peek at these terrific books in next month's LOVESWEPTs. And immediately following this page, look for a preview of the spectacular women's fiction books from Bantam *available now!*

Don't miss these exciting books by your
favorite Bantam authors

On sale in September:
A WHISPER OF ROSES
by Teresa Medeiros

TENDER BETRAYAL
by Rosanne Bittner

THE PAINTED LADY
by Lucia Grahame

OREGON BROWN
by Sara Orwig

And in hardcover from Doubleday
SEIZED BY LOVE
by Susan Johnson

Teresa Medeiros

nationally bestselling author of
ONCE AN ANGEL
and HEATHER AND VELVET

presents

A WHISPER OF ROSES

"From humor to adventure, poignancy to passion, tenderness to sensuality, Teresa Medeiros writes rare love stories to cherish."—*Romantic Times*

Set in the wild Highlands of Scotland, this captivating historical romance is bursting with the breathtaking passion, sparkling humor, and enchanting atmosphere that have made Teresa Medeiros a bestselling author. It tells the heartbreaking tale of two lovers torn between their passion and the clan rivalry that divides their families.

The door behind him crashed open into the opposite wall, and Morgan swung around to find himself facing yet another exotic creature of myth.

A princess, her cloud of dark hair tumbled loose around her shoulders, the light behind her throwing every curve beneath her ivory nightdress into magnificent relief. Her delicate fingers were curled not around a scepter, but around the engraved hilt of a ceremonial claymore.

Silvery fingers of moonlight caressed the five feet of steel that lay between her hands and his heart.

"Hold your ground, rogue MacDonnell," she sweetly snarled. "One careless step and I'll be forced to take your head downstairs without the rest of you."

Morgan didn't even feel the pain as the crystal rose

snapped in his clumsy hands, embedding its stem deep in his palm.

"Why, you clumsy oaf! Look what you've gone and done now!"

Morgan's gaze automatically dropped to his hands. A jagged shard of glass protruded from his palm. Warm blood trickled down his wrist and forearm to puddle on one of Elizabeth Cameron's precious rugs. Before he could quench it, the old shame flared. Shame for being a MacDonnell. Shame for being such a crude ox. Just as quickly on its heels followed rage—the crushing rage that shielded his tattered pride from every blow. But before he could unleash it on the hapless girl, she dropped the sword and rushed over to him.

Tossing the splintered remains of the rose aside without a second glance, she cradled his hand in hers and dabbed at the wound with a wad of her nightdress. Her little hand was warm and soft and silky smooth beneath his own. "You really should take more care," she chided. "If you'd have struck your wrist, you might have bled to death."

Morgan was too dumbfounded by her concern to point out her illogic. If she'd have cut off his head, he might have bled to death even quicker. Still scowling over his hand, she dragged him toward the pale circle of light at the window.

"Be very still," she commanded. "I'm going to try to fish out this piece of glass. It's bound to be painful. You may scream if you like. I shan't think any less of you."

Since she'd never thought much of him to begin with, Morgan wasn't concerned. He didn't even flinch when she pressed his palm with her thumb and snagged the sliver of glass between the polished crescents of her fingernails.

Thoroughly bemused, Morgan studied her in the moonlight. The top of her head barely came to his chest. The spiral curls he used to yank with such relish tumbled down her back in inky waves. Her skin was fair except for the faintest hint of color, as if God had brushed rose petals across her cheeks and lips. A fringe of ebony silk shuttered her eyes. Her scent filled his nostrils, and he was shocked to feel his throat tighten with a primal hunger. She smelled like her mother, but fresher, sweeter. Some primitive male instinct warned him this was a bloom still on the vine, fragrant and tender and ripe. He frowned. She might be nectar to another man, but to him, Dougal Cameron's daughter would be as deadly as nightshade.

Her teeth cut into her lower lip as if to bite back a cry of her own as she drew forth the shard of glass and stanched the bleeding with yet another wad of her nightdress. Morgan feared he might soon have more of it twined around his arm than she had around her body. But an intriguing glimpse of a slender calf silenced his protest.

Grimacing, she lay the bloody splinter on the window-sill before glancing up at him.

At that moment, he cocked his head to the side, giving her an unobstructed view of his face. Moonlight melted over its harsh planes and angles, etching its alien virility in ruthless lines. He was a stranger, yet so hauntingly familiar she couldn't stop her hand from lifting, her fingertips from brushing the stubborn jut of his jaw. His eyes were guarded, like the forest at dusk.

"Hello, brat," he said.

Then she felt that old, familiar kick in the stomach and knew she was standing face to face in the moonlit tower with Morgan MacDonnell, his boyish promise of masculine beauty come to devastating fruition.

Mortified by her own boldness, she snatched her hand back, remembering another time she had touched him in tenderness and he had rubuked her in anger.

A wry grin touched his lips. "I suppose if you'd have known it was me, you'd have let me bleed to death."

Terrified she was going to revert to a stammering six-year-old, she snapped, "Of course not. You were dripping all over Mama's Flemish rug."

To hide her consternation, she lowered her gaze back to his hand. That was a mistake for she could not help staring, fascinated by the blunt size of his fingers, the warmth of his work-roughened skin, the rhythmic throb of his pulse beneath her thumb. She had the absurd thought that it must take a mighty heart indeed to fuel such a man.

"You've grown," she blurted out accusingly.

"So have you."

His low, amused tone warned her. She looked up to find his gaze taking a leisurely jaunt up her body, finally coming to rest with bold regard on her face. A splinter of anger twisted in her heart. For so long she had yearned for him to look at her with affection. But why now, when she sensed his admiration might be even more lethal to her than enmity?

Hardly aware of her actions, she tore a strip of priceless Chinese silk from her mother's drapes and wrapped it around his palm. "So what were you doing up here? Plotting a massacre? Trying to find a way to lower the harpsichord out the window? Searching for a mouse to put in my bed?"

Lucky mouse, Morgan thought, but he wisely refrained from saying so. "If you must know, lass, I was searchin' for a moment's peace."

"Ha!" She knotted the bandage with a crisp jerk that finally drew a flinch from him. "Peace and the MacDonnells hardly go hand in hand."

"Fine talk from a lass who just burst in here threatenin' to cut off my head."

Sabrina could hardly argue with the truth of that.

He jerked his head toward the door. "Why aren't you down there with the rest of your family, lordin' your noble gestures over the poor peasants?"

Morgan's size might have changed, but not the rest of him. Resenting his uncanny knack of making her feel ashamed of who she was, she gave a dainty snort. "Peasants, indeed. Barefoot savages, the lot of them. Mama would have been better off serving them at a trough instead of a table."

His voice was quiet, its very lack of emotion a rebuke of its own. "If their table manners aren't to your likin', it might be because most of them won't see that much food again in their lifetimes. And their feet are bare because they're savin' the rotted soles of their boots for the cold winter months. They don't lose as many toes that way."

Shame buffeted her. Sabrina dropped her gaze, then wished she hadn't as it fell on the stark lines of Morgan's bare legs and feet. Golden hair dusted his muscular calves. His soles must be as tough as leather to bear the stony soil of the mountainside without protection. Her own toes curled sheepishly into the plush cashmere of her stockings.

"I begged Mama to let me join the festivities," she confessed.

"Why didn't you appeal to your dotin' papa? As I recall,

he never could resist a flutter of those pretty little lashes of yours."

Sabrina's gaze shot to his face. Morgan had never given her any indication that he'd noticed her lashes before. "Even Papa was adamant this time." A soft chuckle escaped her. "It seems your reputations preceded you. He was terrified one of you might hit me over the head and drag me off by my hair."

Morgan was silent for so long that she feared she'd offended him again. Then he reached down and lifted a skein of her hair in his uninjured hand, rubbing it between thumb and forefinger. A dreamy languor stole across her features. The cadence of Sabrina's heartbeat shifted in warning.

He let the stolen tendril ripple through his fingers in a cascade of midnight silk before turning the dusky heat of his gaze on her. "I can't say I blame him, lass. If you were mine, I'd probably lock you away, too."

If you were mine . . .

The words hung suspended between them, far more awkward than their silence. In a breath of utter lunacy, Sabrina wondered how it would feel to belong to a man like him, dared to ponder what came after being dragged off by her hair.

Caught in the same spell of moonlight and solitude, Morgan's gaze dropped to her parted lips. His starving senses reeled, intoxicated by the scent of roses that flared his nostrils, the cling of her hair against his callused knuckles. He'd long ago resigned himself to the harsh life of a Highland warrior. But this girl's softness awakened old hungers and weakened his resolve. He hadn't touched a drop of wine, yet he felt drunk, reckless. What harm could one kiss to? Resisting the temptation to plunge his tongue between her unwitting lips, he leaned down and touched his mouth to hers.

At the press of Morgan's lips against her own, Sabrina's eyes fluttered shut. His kiss was brief, dry, almost tentative, yet a melting sweetness unfolded within her. She felt the leashed power in his touch. Such gentleness in a man his size wove a spell all its own. Only in the last brief second of contact did he allow himself the wicked luxury of dragging his lips across hers, molding her beneath him in perfect harmony.

TENDER BETRAYAL
by
ROSANNE BITTNER

Bestselling author of OUTLAW HEARTS
and THUNDER ON THE PLAINS

"Bittner's characters are so finely drawn, their lives so
richly detailed, one cannot help but to care deeply for
each of them." —*Affaire de Coeur*

*When Audra Brennan savored her first, forbidden taste of
desire in the arms of handsome lawyer Lee Jeffreys, his
caresses sparked a flame within that burned away the differ-
ences between rebel and Yankee.*

The shelling from the bigger guns seemed to have
stopped. She decided that at least until daylight she had no
choice but to stay here as Lee had directed. She went back
to the cot and lay down, breathing his scent on his pillow
and sheets. How odd that she felt so safe in this bed where
a Yankee soldier slept. She was in the center of the enemy
camp, yet she was not afraid.

She drifted off to sleep, losing all track of time. Finally
someone knocked gently on the rear door. "Audra? It's
me."

Audra rubbed at her eyes, holding the shirt around
herself as she found her way to the door. It was still dark.
"Lee?"

"Let me in. The worst is over."

Audra obeyed, and Lee turned and latched the door
again. Audra looked up at him, seeing blood on his right
arm. "You're hurt!"

"Nothing drastic. I told my commander I'd tend to it

myself. He doesn't know you're in here, and I don't want him to know just yet." He threw a bundle of clothes on the small table on which the lamp was sitting. "I looted those out of a clothing store like a common thief. I don't know your size. I just took a guess. You've got to have something to wear when you leave here."

Lee removed his jacket and boots, then began unbuttoning his shirt. "It's a madhouse out there. Most of the men have chased the rebels back into the countryside, and they're looting through town like crazy men. It's practically impossible to keep any of these men in line. They aren't regular army, just civilian volunteers, for the most part, come here to teach the rebels a lesson. They don't know a damn thing about real military conduct or how to obey orders." He glanced at her. "I still intend to have the bastards who attacked you whipped. How do you feel?"

She sat down on the cot, suddenly self-conscious now that she was more rested. She had removed her shoes and stockings and wore only his shirt and her bloomers. "Just terribly tired and . . . I don't know . . . numb, I guess. It's all so ugly and unreal."

"That's war, Audra, ugly and unreal. You asked me once what it's like. Now you know." He peeled off his bloodstained shirt, and Audra found herself studying his muscular arms and the familiar broad chest, the dark hair that lightly dusted that chest and led downward in a V shape past the belt of his pants. He walked to the stand that still held a bowl of water and he poured some fresh water into it, then wet a rag and held it to the cut on his arm, which was already scabbing over. "Some rebel tried to stab me with his bayonet. Missed what he was aiming for by a long shot, but he didn't miss me all together, obviously."

"Let me help you."

"Don't worry about it. It isn't bleeding anymore." He washed his face and neck, then dried off and picked up a flask of whiskey. He opened it and poured some over the cut, grimacing at the sting of it. Then he swallowed some of the whiskey straight from the flask. "They say whiskey is supposed to help ease pain," he said then. "It does, but only physical pain. It doesn't do a thing for the pain in a man's heart."

She looked away. "Lee, don't—"

"Why not? In a couple of days you'll go back to Brennan Manor, and I'll go on with what I have to do, because I'm bound to do it and it isn't in me to be a deserter, no matter the reason. You have to stay near home because it's the only way you're going to know what happened to Joey, and you'll want to be there when he comes home, God willing. Who knows what will happen when all this is over? In the meantime I've found you again, and I need to tell you I love you, Audra. I never stopped loving you and I probably never will."

Audra held back tears. Why was he saying this now, when it was impossible for them to be together? Everything had changed. They were not the same people as they'd been that summer at Maple Shadows, and besides that, it was wrong to be sitting here half-undressed in front of the man she'd slept with while married to someone else, wasn't it? It was wrong to care this much about a Yankee. *All* of this was wrong, but then, what was right anymore?

He set the flask down on the table. "This might really be it, Audra; the end for you and me. But we have tonight."

"Why is it always that way for us? It was like that at Maple Shadows, and that one night you came to visit. All we ever have is one night, Lee, never knowing what will come tomorrow. I can't do that again. It hurts too much, and it's wrong."

Audra looked away as Lee began to undress. "Please take me somewhere, Lee, anywhere away from here."

He came over to kneel in front of her, grasping her wrists. "There *is* no place to take you, not tonight. And it's *not* wrong, Audra. It was *never* wrong, and you know it. And this time it isn't just tonight. When this is over, I'm coming back, and we're going to be together, do you hear me? I'm not going to live like this the rest of my life. I want you, Audra, and dammit, you want *me*! We've both known it since that first day you came here to see me, widow or not! Maybe this *is* the last chance we'll have to be together, but as God is my witness, if I don't get killed or so badly wounded that I can't come to you, I'll be back to find you, and we're going to put this war behind us!"

She looked at him pleadingly. "That's impossible now," she said in a near whisper.

"That isn't true. You just don't want to *believe* that it's possible, because it makes you feel like a traitor." He leaned closer. "Well, then, *I'm* a traitor, too! Because while my men are out there chasing and killing rebels, I'll be in here making *love* to one!"

Why couldn't she object, argue, remember why she should say no? Why was she never able to resist this man she should have hated?

"I never said anything about making love," she whispered.

He searched her green eyes, eyes that had told him all along how much she wanted him again. "You didn't have to," he answered.

THE PAINTED LADY
by
LUCIA GRAHAME

This is a stunningly sensual first novel about sexual awakening set in nineteenth-century France and England. Romantic Times called it "a unique and rare reading experience."

This wonderfully entertaining novel showcases the superb writing talents of Lucia Grahame. With lyric simplicity and beauty THE PAINTED LADY will entrance you from first page to last. Read on to discover an exquisite story about a proud, dark-haired woman and her hidden desire that is finally freed.

"If I stay longer with you tonight," Anthony said, his words seeming to reach me through a thick mist, "it will be on one condition. You will not balk at *anything* I ask of you. I leave it to you. I will go now and count tonight to your account, since, although you were occasionally dilatory, you acquitted yourself well enough, for the most part. Or I will stay, on *my* conditions—but at *your* wish. It rests with you. Do I stay or go?"

"Stay," I whispered.

I swayed and jingled as he led me back to the hearthside and laid me down upon the pillows.

"Undress me," he commanded when we were stretched out before the fire. "Slowly. As slowly as you can."

I moved closer to him and began to unfasten the buttons of his waistcoat.

He sighed.

"Don't rush," he whispered. "I can feel how eager you are, but try to control yourself. Take your time."

It was maddening to force myself to that unhurried

pace, but in the end it only sharpened my hunger. As I contemplated the climactic pleasures in store—who could have said how long it would take to achieve them?—I could not help savoring the small but no less sweet ones immediately at hand. The slight drag against my skin of the fine wool that clothed him, more teasing even than I had imagined it; the almost imperceptible fragrance of lavender that wafted from his shirt, the hands which lay so lightly upon my waist as I absorbed the knowledge that the task he had set for me was not an obstacle to fulfillment but a means of enhancing it.

Yet I had unbuttoned only his waistcoat and his shirt when he told me to stop. He drew back from me a little. The very aura of controlled desire he radiated made me long to submerge myself in the impersonal heat and forgetfulness that his still presence next to me both promised and withheld.

I moved perhaps a centimeter closer to him.

"No," he said.

He began, in his calm, unhasty way, to remove his remaining clothing himself. I steadied my breath a little and watched the firelight move like a sculptor's fingers over his cool, hard body.

At last he leaned over me, but without touching me.

"You're so compliant tonight," he said almost tenderly. "You must be very hungry for your freedom, *mon fleur du miel*."

I felt a twist of sadness. For an instant, I thought he had used Frederick's nickname for me. But he had called me something quite different—a flower, not of evil, but of sweetness . . . honey.

He brought his hand to my cheek and stroked it softly. I closed my eyes. Only the sudden sharp intake of my breath could have told him of the effect of that light touch.

He bent his head. I caught the scents of mint and smoke and my own secrets as his mouth moved close to mine.

I tipped my head back and opened my lips.

How long I had resisted those kisses! Now I craved his mouth, wanting to savor and prolong every sensation that could melt away my frozen, imprisoning armor of misery and isolation.

He barely grazed my lips with his.

Then he pulled himself to his knees and gently coaxed me into the same position, facing him.

Keeping his lips lightly on mine, he reached out and took my shoulders gently to bring me closer. My breasts brushed his chest with every long, shivering breath I took.

"You are free now," whispered my husband at last, releasing me, "to do as you like. . . . How will you use your liberty?"

For an answer, I put my arms around his neck, sank back upon the pillows, pulling him down to me, and brought my wild mouth to his. . . .

OREGON BROWN
by
SARA ORWIG

Bestselling author of TIDES OF PASSION
and NEW ORLEANS

"The multi-faceted talent of Sara Orwig gleams as
bright as gold." —*Rave Reviews*

*With more than five million copies of her books in print,
Sara Orwig is without a doubt one of romance's top authors.
Her previous novels have been showered with praise and
awards, including five* Romantic Times *awards and nu-
merous* Affaire de Coeur *awards.*

*Now Bantam Books is proud to present a new edition of one
of her most passionate novels—the story of a woman forced to
choose between fantasy and reality. . . .*

Charity Webster left the city for small-town Oklahoma
to assume the reins of the family company she had
inherited. With nothing behind her but a failed business and a shattered romance, and no one in her new
life except an aging aunt, Charity gives her nights to a
velvet-voiced late-night deejay . . . and to a fantasy
about the man behind the sexy, sultry voice.

But daylight brings her into head-on conflict with
another man, the wealthy O. O. Brown, who is maneu-
vering to acquire the family firm. Arrogant and all too
aware of his own charm, he still touches off a sensuous
spark in Charity that she can't deny . . . and she finds
herself torn between two men—one a mystery, the
other the keeper of her deepest secrets.

And don't miss these heart-stopping
romances from Bantam Books,
on sale in October:

OUTLAW by Susan Johnson

MOONLIGHT, MADNESS,
AND MAGIC
by Suzanne Forster,
Charlotte Hughes,
and Olivia Rupprecht

SATIN AND STEELE
by Fayrene Preston

And in hardcover from Doubleday:

SOMETHING BORROWED,
SOMETHING BLUE
by Gillian Karr

OFFICIAL RULES

To enter the sweepstakes below carefully follow all instructions found elsewhere ir this offer.

The **Winners Classic** will award prizes with the following approximate maximum values: 1 Grand Prize: $26,500 (or $25,000 cash alternate); 1 First Prize: $3,000; Second Prizes: $400 each; 35 Third Prizes: $100 each; 1,000 Fourth Prizes: $7.50 each Total maximum retail value of Winners Classic Sweepstakes is $42,500. Some presentations of this sweepstakes may contain individual entry numbers correspond ing to one or more of the aforementioned prize levels. To determine the Winners individual entry numbers will first be compared with the winning numbers preselecte by computer. For winning numbers not returned, prizes will be awarded in random drawings from among all eligible entries received. Prize choices may be chosen a various levels. If a winner chooses an automobile prize, all license and registratio fees, taxes, destination charges all, and, other expenses not offered herein are the responsibility of the winner. If a winner chooses a trip, travel must be complete withir one year from the time the prize is awarded. Minors must be accompanied by an adul Travel companion(s) must also sign release of liability. Trips are subject to space an departure availability. Certain black-out dates may apply.

The following applies to the sweepstakes named above:

No purchase necessary. You can also enter the sweepstakes by sending your nam and address to: P.O. Box 508, Gibbstown, N.J. 08027. Mail each entry separately Sweepstakes begins 6/1/93. Entries must be received by 12/30/94. Not responsibl for lost, late, damaged, misdirected, illegible or postage due mail. Mechanicall reproduced entries are not eligible. All entries become property of the sponsor an will not be returned.

Prize Selection/Validations: Selection of winners will be conducted no later tha 5:00 PM on January 28, 1995, by an independent judging organization whose decision are final. Random drawings will be held at 1211 Avenue of the Americas, New Yor N.Y. 10036. Entrants need not be present to win. Odds of winning are determine by total number of entries received. Circulation of this sweepstakes is estimated n to exceed 200 million. All prizes are guaranteed to be awarded and delivered t winners. Winners will be notified by mail and may be required to complete an affidavi of eligibility and release of liability which must be returned within 14 days of date o notification or alternate winners will be selected in a random drawing. Any priz notification letter or any prize returned to a participating sponsor, Bantam Doubleda Dell Publishing Group, Inc., its participating divisions or subsidiaries, or th independent judging organization as undeliverable will be awarded to an alternat winner. Prizes are not transferable. No substitution for prizes except as offered or i may be necessary due to unavailability, in which case a prize of equal or greater valu will be awarded. Prizes will be awarded approximately 90 days after the drawing. A taxes are the sole responsibility of the winners. Entry constitutes permission (exce where prohibited by law) to use winners' names, hometowns, and likenesses f publicity purposes without further or other compensation. Prizes won by minors w be awarded in the name of parent or legal guardian.

Participation: Sweepstakes open to residents of the United States and Canad except for the province of Quebec. Sweepstakes sponsored by Bantam Doubleda Dell Publishing Group, Inc., (BDD), 1540 Broadway, New York, NY 10036. Versio of this sweepstakes with different graphics and prize choices will be offered conjunction with various solicitations or promotions by different subsidiaries ar divisions of BDD. Where applicable, winners will have their choice of any pri offered at level won. Employees of BDD, its divisions, subsidiaries, advertisir agencies, independent judging organization, and their immediate family members a not eligible.

Canadian residents, in order to win, must first correctly answer a time limite arithmetical skill testing question. Void in Puerto Rico, Quebec and wherev prohibited or restricted by law. Subject to all federal, state, local and provincial la and regulations. For a list of major prize winners (available after 1/29/95): send a se addressed, stamped envelope entirely separate from your entry to: Sweepstak Winners, P.O. Box 517, Gibbstown, NJ 08027. Requests must be received by 12/30/94. D NOT SEND ANY OTHER CORRESPONDENCE TO THIS P.O. BOX.

SWP 7/

Don't miss these fabulous Bantam women's fiction titles on sale in October

• OUTLAW

by Susan Johnson, author of SINFUL & FORBIDDEN

From the supremely talented mistress of erotic historical romance comes a sizzling love story of a fierce Scottish border lord who abducts his sworn enemy, a beautiful English woman — only to find himself a captive of her love.

_____29955-7 $5.50/6.50 in Canada

• MOONLIGHT, MADNESS, AND MAGIC

by Suzanne Forster, Charlotte Hughes, and Olivia Rupprecht

Three romantic supernatural novellas set in 1785, 1872, and 1992. "Incredibly ingenious." — Romantic Times
"Something for everyone." — Gothic Journal
"An engaging read." — Publishers Weekly
"Exemplary." — Rendezvous   _____56052-2 $5.50/6.50 in Canada

• SATIN AND STEELE

by Fayrene Preston, co-author of THE DELANEY CHRISTMAS CAROL

Fayrene Preston's classic tale of a woman who thought she could never love again, and a man who thought love had passed him by.   _____56457-9 $4.50/5.50 in Canada

Ask for these books at your local bookstore or use this page to order.